A Christmas Most Shocking

A Harry Reese Mystery

For a glossary of period terms, biographies of the characters, and a complete chronology, please visit:

HarryReeseMysteries.com

A Christmas Most Shocking

Robert Bruce Stewart

Street Car Mysteries

Florence, Mass.

First Print Edition, November 2017

ISBN 978-1-938710-30-8

Street Car Mysteries

streetcarmysteries.com

To those oddities among us who began as little girls

Part I

The Account of Harry Reese

1

It was dark as the proverbial pitch when my outstretched hand came upon a certain bit of female anatomy only notionally concealed beneath a sweep of sheer silk lingerie. I braced for some remonstration, but heard only a sharp inhalation followed by an enigmatic moan.

"Is that you, Emmie?" I asked.

"Yes.... Yes, darling, it's me," she said breathlessly. "Go on back to bed and I'll be with you shortly."

I felt her face near mine; she planted a soft kiss on my cheek, her tongue pressing delicately against my flesh.

There were three strong reasons for suspecting this woman was not Emmie. First, Emmie had never in my presence used the word darling, breathlessly or otherwise. Second, the last time she'd donned nightwear of that nature, she was more than four years younger and four cocktails more suggestible. Third, this mystery woman bore a distinctive scent—subtle, but undeniably inciting. Emmie never wore scent. The truth is, I had only addressed her as Emmie to use my apparent misunderstanding as an excuse for having taken liberties with her certain bit of anatomy.

Nonetheless, the soft kiss and delicate tongue quite effectively extinguished these doubts—as well as all others not enumerated. If this woman was under the impression she was Emmie, her word was good enough for me. I felt my way back to our darkened room and into bed.

"Where were you?" Emmie asked.

"Out looking for you." Just then, the light on her side of the bed came on. "Someone must have replaced the fuse."

"I thought you were asleep."

"I was, until the light went out."

"Why would the light going out wake you up?" she asked, naively.

"Opportunity. You don't like me to disturb your reading. I thought you'd turned it off. Where'd you go?"

"To see about the lights. I was in the middle of the last chapter.... But it was too dark to see, so I just came back to bed."

"I don't see how I missed you."

"I needed to deliver a message to Señor Garcia—if you must know."

This is Emmie's preferred euphemism for the euphemism "to see a man about a dog."

"Just so it wasn't to a Frenchman," I said, more or less under my breath.

"Captain Dumont? What are you talking about?"

"Let's just say there are rumors."

"Rumors? Don't talk such nonsense, Harry." She picked up her book, then set it down again. "I wonder what would have blown a fuse at one in the morning?"

"In this house, I'd be afraid to ask. Say, whatever happened to that silk negligee of yours?"

"Which one? The one I bought last week is in the wardrobe."

Bought last week? Interesting she'd purchased a new silk negligee in December, and while she expected to be traveling alone.

"Why don't you try it on for me?"

2

"Forget it, Harry. I'm going to finish my book. Good night."

It wasn't until late the next morning we learned the precise cause of the outage. It involved a frayed lamp cord, a precariously positioned pitcher of water, and a visiting member of the German aristocracy.

The death of the Count von Schnurrenberger und Kesselheim was every bit as suspicious—and almost as inglorious—as that of his uncle and immediate predecessor, an ill-omened soul who'd choked to death on a chicken bone concealed in his Charlotte Russe. That unfortunate accident had occurred five years earlier.

There were a number of other parallels as well. Both were proud men of military bearing who displayed qualities likely to provoke the passions in others—and not incidentally, the dueling scars to prove it. What's more, each met his demise while residing in Washington, the latest count just a few days before Christmas 1906. Lastly, both had recently fallen out of favor with a certain former jewel thief, a petite woman with red hair and freckles, known in her criminal past as Madame B_____, and, after marrying the previous count, simply as "the countess." It was in her well-appointed home that Emmie and I were then staying and the count met his untimely end. But, as I mentioned earlier, we only learned of that tragedy late that morning.

Breakfast at the countess's was an informal affair, laid out on the sideboard in the large dining room. When Emmie and I came down, Captain Dumont was seated by himself at one end of the long table. He rose when we entered and gave us, or Emmie at least, a slight bow.

I'd met the unctuous knave only the day before, on my arrival from Brooklyn—but the animus had come packed in my bag. He was an officer of engineers detailed to the French Embassy as an aide to the military attaché. He stood about six feet tall, and the uniform, I had to admit, fit him nicely. Why is it every suit of clothes seems tailored specifically for unctuous knaves?

He was probably about thirty, nearer to Emmie's age. When we'd all sat down, the two of them began speaking in French. I only caught every third word or so, as I'm sure he expected. The conversation seemed to center on the outage and what might have been the cause. Then the talk veered to other topics, the nature of which I couldn't comprehend. The only hint was that at the conclusion of some comment of Emmie's, Captain Dumont glanced in my direction and inquired incredulously, "*Celui-là?*" Emmie shrugged, and almost stifled a laugh. He joined her, with no pretense of stifling. I conjectured the odds of successfully hiding a chicken bone in his eggs and made a mental note to bring one to breakfast on the morrow.

Suddenly, Sesbania entered the room—which seemed to be her manner in all things. She was a girl of ten or eleven who was staying with the countess while her parents were traveling in Europe. Given my treatment at the table, I welcomed her company—guardedly.

"Would you like more coffee?" she asked me.

"That would be nice. Could you ask the maid?"

"Oh, yes. Provided…" She held up a tin can decorated in colorful paper and shook it so the coins inside jingled.

"Look," I said. "I've been here less than a day and I've already contributed a dollar to Mrs. What's-her-name's defense fund."

"Mrs. Bradley. And a dollar won't go far in a murder trial."

"Murder? You didn't mention murder. Who's she accused of killing?"

"A former senator. Mr. Brown of Utah."

"And you're convinced she didn't do it?"

"Oh, she shot him, of course. But only because he refused to marry her."

"And that amounts to justifiable homicide in the District of Columbia?"

"When a man uses a woman the way he did...." She slowly shook her head as she spoke.

"What would you know about that?"

"Well, there are children...." Now she raised her eyebrows, just in case I needed help in making the proper inference.

"You shouldn't be allowed to read newspapers."

"For goodness' sake, Harry," Emmie interjected. "Give the child a dime."

"A quarter," the little extortionist corrected. "Tradesmen may contribute a dime, but guests are generally happy to contribute a quarter, at the very least. Captain Dumont always contributes a whole franc."

"You've been had. That's just twenty cents in coin of the realm. And why should I give you a quarter to call the maid when I could go out and *buy* the coffee for a nickel?"

"Not in this neighborhood. And you'd likely find yourself contributing just the same. Suppose you needed help in finding your overcoat? *It's awfully cold outside this morning.*"

"You hid my overcoat?"

"I may have done some straightening up of the hall closet. Mother made me promise I would help about the house."

I tossed her a quarter. Before she'd even turned to leave, the maid arrived with a fresh pot of coffee. Her name was Geneviève. She smiled at me as she poured. I was comforted at having found one genuinely friendly face. The evening before she'd brought me a towel, then lingered to ask about my trip. A congenial girl.

At last, our hostess entered the room. Dumont rose and made another little bow. So then I had to rise as well—but I drew the line at bowing.

Emmie and I were well acquainted with the countess, having met her on a previous trip to the city around the time of her husband's death. We'd met an even younger—but no less artful—version of Sesbania during the same visit. I'd come to Washington investigating several fraudulent insurance claims, a case that ultimately involved two murders—not even including the ill-fated count's assignation with the chicken bone.

What name the dowager countess held originally, I can't say. The only hint of her past she'd disclosed in my hearing was the dubious assertion that her father was some sort of free-lance swineherd in Shropshire, an expert at raising very fat pigs. But the sum of her talents argued against so humble an origin.

She spoke several languages fluently and was the consummate conversationalist in each of them. Always witty, affable when she wanted, and even—though most rarely, and perhaps never sincerely—a dispenser of flattery, the lady had honed charm into a dangerous weapon. This—combined with an exquisite taste in wardrobe and accoutrement, and in spite of her modest stature—allowed the countess to easily dominate any gathering.

When she wanted to. For most remarkable of all,

with a few slight changes in attire and deportment, she could just as easily recede into the crowd unnoticed. In this regard, she was quite chameleon-like. A useful talent for a woman of intrigue—or a master jewel thief.

She had been much younger than her former husband. Even now, five years after his death, she couldn't have been much over thirty. He had been attached to the German Embassy in Washington, and after his death, she stayed on. Her present home had been purchased from a popular hostess. That lady had used it to house an exclusive poolroom, a place where the elites of the capital could place bets on the horse races taking place in cities across the East. The countess had apparently discontinued that enterprise, but still entertained frequently and lavishly.

She had made clear on my arrival that I was admitted reluctantly. It was Emmie she had invited, ostensibly to begin work as her official biographer. She had made a similar offer five years earlier, only to withdraw it later when Emmie had proven insufficiently obsequious.

The rest of us sat in silence while the countess attended her newspaper assiduously and her breakfast indifferently. She was not one to squander her vivacity on the breakfast table.

I was about to excuse myself when we heard excited voices upstairs. A few moments later, Thomas—the countess's loyal factotum—descended and approached his mistress. He stood by at attention until she eventually set down the newspaper and looked at him. He leaned down and whispered something in her ear, then resumed his upright pose as if awaiting instructions.

"Damn," his mistress expostulated. "How typically ungrateful of him."

"What is it?" Emmie asked.

"That fool, the count. Evidently, he electrocuted himself in his bed last night."

"*Il s'est électrocuté?*" the Frenchman asked.

"*Oui.*"

"But that's not possible...." Dumont told her.

"You'll have to argue that point with the corpse. I suppose we'll need to call a doctor."

"His valet suspects murder, madam," Thomas told her.

"How absurd. I never liked that shifty valet. Probably scheming to extort money from me somehow. Go and fetch Dr. Gillette, Thomas. Don't telephone, take the auto. Drag him here, if you have to. I think we can trust his discretion."

You may take it on faith she trusted his discretion only because she had evidence of some indiscretion on his part. The countess's objections to extortion were by no means categorical.

She glanced across the table at Captain Dumont. He wasn't looking nearly so smug as he had a little earlier. A little squeamish, I thought, for a military man. Then her eyes fell on me.

"Make yourself useful, Harry. Go up and look into it. You seem to have an affinity for corpses." It was the first time she'd called me by name since greeting me on my arrival. I say greeting, though cautioning would be closer to the mark.

"All right." I started on my way, but as I passed, she grabbed my sleeve and pulled me down beside her.

"I'd be most appreciative, Harry," she whispered, "if we can remove all doubt about it being an accident." She smiled at me, then, after releasing my sleeve, ran her slender fingers along the back of my hand.

I looked over at Emmie. She was fittingly non-plussed. Served her right.

"I'll come, too," she said.

"No," the countess told her. "You'll stay here with me."

Upstairs in the count's room, I found the valet on his knees. He'd unplugged the cord of a table lamp and was examining it.

"Frayed?" I asked.

"Yes, it is."

We introduced ourselves. Otto Kirsch was a fellow of medium height with a thin mustache and a thick accent. His master, the count, was slumped over in bed with a look of surprise permanently affixed to his face. The linen and his nightshirt were soaking wet. A glass pitcher was on the bed beside him, unbroken but empty. Lying on the floor was a small lamp. I could see at once that the bed-side table they'd apparently been resting on sat unevenly.

"The count must not have realized how unsteady the table was," I said. "It wouldn't have taken more than a bump to cause the pitcher to spill. Then the frayed cord did the rest."

"*If*," the valet stipulated, "the table had been unsteady."

"You can see for yourself." I used a finger to shift it back and forth.

"Yes, but look down here."

I got down on my hands and knees beside him. Under the bed, about a foot away from the table, was a small square of wood. He slid it under the short leg of the table. It fit perfectly.

"Well, that just explains why he hadn't noticed before. Someone must have put that there as a fix. Then in bumping the table, the count knocked it off the shim."

"No, you need to look more closely."

He held up the block of wood. There was a thin silk string, like fishing line, attached to it. He handed it to me.

"Pull on it."

I did so, but though the silk line gave, it was only with some resistance. As if I was working against a spring.

"It leads along the floor to behind that chest of drawers."

It took the two of us to slide it away from the wall.

"Look," he said, pointing.

Attached to the back of the dresser were two pairs of pulleys. Between them hung a large weight, like that from a sash window. Two lines were attached to the weight, each drawing over two of the pulleys. The first led to the block of wood, and the other to a small door used by the servants. It was open and the valet closed it. This drew up the weight. Next he went over and positioned the block of wood under the shortened leg, then placed the pitcher atop the now steady table. He walked back and reopened the door.

As he did so, the weight descended, and as it did, it pulled the line connected to the block of wood supporting the table. Before the door was even half open, the pitcher had fallen back onto the bed.

"We must call the police, immediately," he said.

As beguiling as I found the countess—all right, frightening—it seemed a rather tall order to refashion the scene into a convincing case of accidental death. Especially without the connivance of the valet. And he seemed that rare sort of servant who maintains a modicum of loyalty to his employer, even posthumously. Our own maid was probably absconding with our few valuables at that very moment, and we were merely out of town.

Still, I wasn't looking forward to sharing my conclusion with the dowager herself. She was almost assuredly going to be of the opinion that I had failed her. And she was the type of woman who held vengeance in high regard. Just how ruthless she really was, I couldn't say. But I did know that the French cook who had prepared the previous count's Charlotte Russe was currently employed in her kitchen.

While I was mulling my predicament, Thomas arrived with Dr. Gillette. We exchanged greetings. He too had been involved with the case that prompted our visit back in 1901. He went over to the body and examined it thoroughly.

"There are no marks of any kind. I think we may assume he died of cardiac arrest."

"Brought on by electric shock?" I showed him the frayed lamp cord.

"I see no evidence of that. There are no burns. It would take an autopsy to be definite.... And I don't think the countess..."

"That will be for the police to decide," the valet interjected.

"Police? But surely, even if electrocution were possible on so little current—which I don't believe it is—it was a simple accident. The wet clothes... the frayed cord..."

The valet brought him over and pointed to the back of the bureau.

"Do you think that was created by accident, Doctor?"

Gillette looked at me nervously. He swallowed, then licked his lips.

"I... I know nothing of mechanics," he said. Then he smiled, weakly. "I'm afraid I must leave it to you to explain this to the countess. She seemed rather adamant that it was an accident."

"But certainly you must remain here until the police arrive," Kirsch insisted.

"I would, of course... but old Mrs. Jenks... I was on my way there when summoned by the countess.... Can I get out this way?" Without waiting for an answer, he exited via the small door and scampered down the back stairs.

"Coward," the valet concluded. "Come, we will inform the countess."

I seriously considered following the doctor's lead, but then noticed Thomas eyeing me as if he had read my thoughts.

2

Kirsch closed and locked both doors of the count's bedroom. Then he, Thomas, and I went downstairs, where the valet approached the lady of the house.

"Well?" she asked, and not at all amiably.

"The count was murdered. There is no question. I will now send for the police."

"Harry!" she somehow shouted through clenched teeth. "What nonsense is this?"

"Ah, I'm afraid it looks rather... Well, I don't think there's much doubt...."

"Quit mumbling! Thomas?"

"I regret to say, it is so, madam."

"Damn. Who then should we call?" she asked rhetorically. No doubt she was running through names of officials she had some dirt on.

"Sergeant Lacy!" Emmie cried.

"Who is Sergeant Lacy?" the countess asked.

"A policeman here. Harry and I met him on our previous visit. He'd be just the man for a case like this."

The countess turned from Emmie to me. "*Is* he the man we want, Harry?"

"Well, I don't think we could do better."

"Then you telephone him. And if he gives you any guff, tell him my friend Commissioner Macfarland will be attending festivities here New Year's Eve."

As Thomas was leading me to the telephone, Sesbania interposed.

"Where's Dr. Gillette?"

"Ah... I believe he left via the rear entrance."

"Without his overcoat and hat?"

"Maybe he couldn't afford to redeem them."

"That's all right. Mr. Serby will be glad to."

"Mr. Serby?"

"He runs a secondhand clothing store downtown. He says that, this time of year, he can use all the overcoats he can get his hands on. He's been very generous toward the fund. Shall I see if I can find yours? I mean, before it becomes *hopelessly* lost."

"How much?"

"Well, it's practically new, isn't it? I'd think it would be easily worth a silver dollar...."

"Yes, I'm sure you would. All right, but after this no more contributions to Mrs. Bradley's defense fund. Agreed?"

"Yes, agreed."

I gave up the silver, but she'd acquiesced too readily to allow me any comfort.

On our prior visit, Detective Sergeant Lacy and I had both been investigating a string of burglaries involving expensive jewelry. When I determined that three of the claims were fraudulent, Lacy lost interest in the case. He was disinclined to press charges against well-connected personages that might not stick. Which is exactly why Emmie suggested him. An unapologetic careerist who could be counted on not to incommode a friend of Commissioner Macfarland was just the sort of policeman the countess wished for.

I reached the sergeant with little trouble. He promised to be there within the hour. I returned and informed the countess.

"And I think it would be best if none of us go out until he arrives. That includes the servants."

"Not even a quick trip to Mr. Serby's store?" Sesbania asked.

"I'm afraid you'll have to put off fencing your booty until later."

"Fencing my booty?"

"Redeeming the doctor's contribution." I looked about the room. "Where's Captain Dumont?"

"Gone home," the countess said.

"To the embassy?"

"To France. His boat sails from New York tomorrow morning."

"That's going to look a little suspicious."

"Don't be an ass. He isn't on the run. His return was planned weeks ago. Didn't you notice his things in the hall?"

"No, I didn't. Sergeant Lacy might insist on wiring ahead and having him held."

"He carries a diplomatic passport. Sergeant Lacy had better think twice before doing anything so foolish. As a matter of fact, *I* insist that we make no mention of Captain Dumont until his boat has safely left port."

"That is unthinkable!" Kirsch told her. "You seem, madam, to take a rather cavalier attitude toward the murder of a guest in your home."

The countess stood up. "Are you implying I had something to do with this?"

"No. Certainly not." The now-unemployed valet seemed suddenly unsure of his ground. "It is only that a gentleman in my care has been murdered. My honor depends on seeing that the culprit is brought to justice."

"Well, just remember: this is *my* home. I suppose the sergeant must be told about Captain Dumont. But I can attest to his whereabouts when the lights went out."

With that, she glided into the hall and up the stairs.

Kirsch stood frozen a moment, then smiled at me and shrugged. When he noticed Emmie watching him, he blushed. "I should go upstairs and guard the room until the sergeant arrives," he told us. He clicked his heels and went into the servants' hall, apparently planning to use the back stairs and thereby avoid any chance encounter with the countess.

Emmie and I appeared to be alone. I poured myself some coffee and sat down. "I suppose that explains why Captain Dumont wasn't staying at the embassy."

"I suppose.... What was it you found upstairs?"

I described the scene, and the complicated device attached to the bureau. And how the door from the servants' hall had been made into a trigger. "It was really very clever. I doubt there are many people who could have come up with it."

"Would it take an engineer?"

"A French engineer? No, I could have worked it out if I put my mind to it."

"It's easy enough to say so now."

"Next time we visit your family, I'll prove it. There's also Madame B_____, of course. She's constructed devices just as complex."

"But not for murder."

"Tastes can change."

"Who's Madame B_____?" a new voice asked.

Emmie shot six inches straight up before descending back into her chair. Suddenly, Sesbania had reappeared.

"Oh... A famous jewel thief, many years back, in Europe. Harry wrote about her in a treatise on burglary."

"I wonder if the countess knew her. She's traveled all over Europe, you know."

"Oh, I wouldn't bother the countess...."

Sesbania held up a little box. Like the can she used to collect for the murderess, it was covered in colored paper. She shook it so we couldn't mistake her intention.

"I thought we agreed," I said. "That silver dollar was it."

"Oh, this isn't for Mrs. Bradley. This is for the Strothers."

"Who are they?"

"Two brothers in Culpepper, Virginia, who shot their sister's husband on his wedding day. A man named Bywaters."

"Well, depending on the temperament of their sister, I guess that might qualify as a mercy killing. Did they have any reason in particular? Poor table manners? Dull conversationalist?"

"He had used their sister badly...." She shook her head slowly, just as she had when recounting the case of Mrs. Bradley.

"Oh. Hadn't he made amends by marrying her?"

"To an extent. But immediately after the ceremony, he tried to escape. And *her* still ill in bed."

"What was she suffering from?" Emmie asked.

"Well... Bywaters, before he married her, had taken her to Washington for what's known as an *illegal operation*."

"Illegal operation?"

"They don't say what it was exactly. But I get the feeling everyone knows but me. What do you think?"

"I... Well... Let's see...." Emmie stuttered to a stop. Once again, she was looking nonplussed.

"Sounds like a tooth extraction by an unlicensed dentist gone bad," I told the girl. "That back-alley work is prone to infection."

"Anyway, something went wrong and now she's recovering in bed." She shook her box.

I tossed her a quarter and was relieved to hear the bell ring. I reached the hall just as Thomas was opening the door to Detective Sergeant Lacy. He took off his coat, hat, and scarf and handed them to the servant.

"Well, Mr. Reese, here we are again. And it sounds like another thorny situation." He peered over my shoulder. "Oh, and I see you've brought your stenographer with you. Miss McGregor, wasn't it?"

"It's McGinnis," I corrected. "Or rather, was. We're married."

"Ah. Made an honest woman of the lady. Good for you, Mr. Reese."

The truth is, we were married last time we met Lacy. But after Emmie told him she was my stenographer—and he subsequently realized she knew nothing of shorthand—he became convinced she traveled with me as my paramour.

Emmie came in with Sesbania.

"That's a beautiful overcoat," the child noted.

"An early Christmas present from the missus."

"Don't even think about it," I told her.

"What's that?" he asked.

"Nothing. Shall we go upstairs?"

"By all means, Mr. Reese. Lead the way. Are you here on another insurance case?"

"No, just... celebrating the holidays with our dear friend, the countess."

The door of the count's room was locked, but on

hearing us, Kirsch opened it from inside. I introduced them.

"The count's valet," Lacy repeated. "And you've been alone in here? I don't like that. No, I don't like that at all."

"What exactly are you implying, Sergeant? I am not used to being distrusted."

"Aren't you, now?" Lacy looked over his shoulder at me and winked.

A key element of the sergeant's investigative technique was to focus suspicions on the most vulnerable person present, a servant preferably, and the darker the complexion the better. Before this was over, I suspected, Kirsch would be regretting his insistence that the police be called in. As things turned out, however, that would be the least of his concerns.

Lacy walked over to the late count. "You said on the telephone Dr. Gillette was here."

"I said, *had* been here. He needed to attend to an emergency."

"Did he, now." Lacy pored over the scene without touching anything, first the bed, then, on his knees, the floor. He rose. "All right, let's see this contraption."

Kirsch showed him his discovery on the back of the bureau. It seemed to perplex the detective, so the valet gave him a demonstration.

"And it was you who discovered it?" Lacy asked him.

"Yes, it was me."

"And why would a murderer expose his own crime? Well, let me tell you, Herr Kirsch, cleverer men than you have tried the same thing. A ripe old chestnut. Eh, Mr. Reese?"

"Is it? Sounds like a chancy strategy."

The sergeant ignored my remark. "When did you last see your employer?" he asked Kirsch.

"I drew him a bath after dinner, as always—at ten o'clock. The count was of impeccable habits. He made a point of always being presentable."

"And who was he presenting himself to last night?"

"I know nothing of that. The count valued discretion above all else."

"Well, Herr Kirsch, the count is dead and I'm running the show here. And there's no place for discretion in a murder investigation. You made a suggestion, now talk."

"I know only that the count was... popular with the ladies."

"But which lady in particular?"

"That, I am afraid, is just it. The count wasn't very particular."

"Well, how many ladies are in the house?"

"Just three, if we don't count the little girl: the countess, her maid Geneviève, and Mrs. Reese."

"*Should* we count the little girl?"

"Certainly not! The count was not a monster. He merely... partook of what was offered."

"Men like that leave a lot of jealous women in their wake...."

"The count, I believe, preferred ladies of an equally... shall we say, cosmopolitan disposition."

"Did he, now? And what about their husbands?"

"That may be a more likely prospect."

"Is it, Herr Kirsch? Then tell me, who is it you suspect?"

"I have no evidence, but..."

"But what?"

"Captain Dumont, a French officer who had been staying here, left rather abruptly after the count was discovered."

"Well, well. That *is* interesting. Left for where?"

"For France. The countess said he will be sailing from New York tomorrow."

"You made no mention of this Frenchman, Mr. Reese."

"I was unaware of his departure when we spoke on the phone. The countess informs me it had been planned for some weeks."

"I see. All right, Herr Kirsch, you may go. But don't leave the house without my permission."

The valet clicked his heels and left via the servants' door.

"Well, well, Mr. Reese. I can see now why you called me in. Quite an interesting case, for sure."

"Downright Holmesian," I said. I'd remembered the sergeant thought himself something of a colleague to the Baker Street sleuth.

"Yes. Yes, indeed. Holmesian is just the word." I'd pleased him. "I called the police surgeon before I left. He should be here soon. Do you think there's somewhere in the house from which I might conduct my investigation? A study?"

"There's the countess's study, but I think she'd object rather strenuously. How about the billiard room?"

"That will do nicely.... Now, what's that?"

He went over to the bed. Lying on the quilt, a foot or so from the count's lap, was a small book. He picked it up. "Must be what he was reading. What do you make of it?" He held it out to me.

"French. I don't recognize the author. A clue?"

"Bah. It wasn't reading that killed him." He tossed the book back on the bed. "This is a case which will turn on motive. All else is distraction. Still, we had better look about the room."

We went through the bureau, the wardrobe, and the writing table and found nothing of particular interest. His correspondence was all routine—positively mundane for a man known to be popular with the ladies. There were about two dozen books, all in either German or French, but none with which I was familiar.

Lacy pulled out his watch. "Half past twelve. Eh, what time is lunch served?"

"I can't really say. I just arrived yesterday. But why don't I arrange to have something brought to the billiard room?"

"That would be ideal. And will you join me? I have a proposition for you."

"A proposition? How intriguing. You'll find the billiard room just off the parlor. I'll go down the back way and talk to the cook."

"Good."

I went down to the kitchen and found the cook as inscrutable as the count's book. He spoke not a word of English, so I conveyed the request to Geneviève. In the hall, I found Lacy with the police surgeon; we escorted him upstairs. On examining the body, he confirmed what Dr. Gillette had said: cardiac arrest, possibly caused by electrocution.

On the way down, we encountered the men who'd come to take away the body. Since I was in the rear, I led them back to the room. One man tossed off the quilt and the little book fell at my feet. I retrieved it. *Gamiani*, it was called. There was an inscription in a perfect hand: *In anticipation*. It also bore a distinctive—now familiar—scent.... I put the little book in my pocket.

Out in the hall, I heard a clatter emanating from our room. Emmie had converted the dressing table into a typing desk and I found her busily pounding the machine's keys.

"How's the investigation going?" There was no cessation to the banging, nor did she look up. Half my conversations with Emmie were over a banging typewriter.

"Just as I'm sure you expected. Lacy wasted no time in accusing the valet."

"There *is* something suspicious about him. I... Damn!" She took a pencil to her page, then went back to typing. "Was there something you wanted?"

"Only to tell you I'll be having lunch in the billiard room with Sergeant Lacy."

"How nice for you. *Bon appétit*."

I left her without replying. Her interest in the case seemed lacking. When we first met, Emmie couldn't get enough of murder. Then her writing took precedence over all else. A year before, she vowed never to be dragged into another what she termed unsenseless murder. By which she meant the murder of someone who was simply getting his just deserts. Did this mean she felt the count deserved *his* death?

Emmie had come down to Washington a fortnight before me, just after the conclusion of a notorious murder trial she was covering for an English newspaper—either the *Bacup Times* or the *Leek Times and Cheadle News*; I often confuse those venerated journals. Perhaps something occurred during the intervening two weeks which placed the count low in her regard. Low enough to kill him? I thought that unlikely, particularly given the means used. To Emmie, physics was a science of the occult.

"Lunch will be served shortly," I told Lacy on entering the billiard room.

He was erasing the slate used to keep score.

"Excellent, Mr. Reese. Now I expect you are wondering as to the nature of my proposition."

"Your proposition? Oh, yes. On tenterhooks."

"Well, given that you are vacationing here, with, I suspect, little else to do, how would you feel about acting as my recorder?"

"Recorder?"

"You see, Mr. Reese, I've solved a great many crimes over the years, some as curious as anything Mr. Holmes has come across...."

"Ah, you need a Watson."

"Precisely. A Watson is exactly what I need. I offered the post to a stenographer, colored, but the ignorant know-nothing turned me down! All because his pay would have fallen four dollars a week."

"Hmm. The venal sort, this stenographer, colored." In Washington, the supplemental appellation was requisite for octoroons on up. "Meanwhile, there's Dr. Watson, willing to set aside his nascent medical practice and traipse around the damp, forbidding moors on the off chance Holmes will spring for lunch."

As if on cue, Geneviève arrived with our sandwiches and two large glasses of pilsner.

"Sandwiches?" Lacy asked with some surprise.

"*Mais oui*. What Monsieur Reese requested, is it not?"

"Yes, I thought it quicker."

She smiled and gave me a wink as she left.

3

The sergeant gave his full attention to his meal and it was only when he'd finished the last of the sandwiches that he returned to the next-most-pressing matter on the agenda: his legacy.

"If you remember, Mr. Reese, Dr. Watson writes mostly from recollection. He has a remarkable memory for detail."

"Almost suspiciously so," I added.

"Yes, exactly. The secret must lie in his note taking. Though he rarely makes mention of it, we must assume note taking is an integral part of the process. Are you prepared to take notes, Mr. Reese?"

"Just let me fetch my notebook."

"Quickly, now. We must strike while the iron is hot."

Provided, apparently, the iron striking doesn't interfere with the meal taking.

In the parlor, Emmie, Sesbania, and the countess were moving about the large tree positioning the customary baubles and garlands. Given the season, there was nothing suspicious in this—except that the tree had already been so adorned on my arrival. They'd been speaking in whispers when I opened the door. Now, all three went quiet and turned my way. I'm not fond of conspiracies generally, but the fact that three of the most treacherous females I'd yet encountered were in secret conference sent a cold chill down my spine.

Emmie's machinations are myriad, but only sometimes dangerous for yours truly (a nasty episode involving a dagger-wielding highbinder and a jar of pickled lambs' tongues comes quickly to mind). The countess, though not so scattershot in her scheming, was considered capable of almost anything—provided she felt her actions justified. (A pointless stipulation, one might argue, since she rarely felt otherwise.) Lastly came Sesbania, whom the countess seemed to have taken on as acolyte. A mere child, but pound-for-pound perhaps the most pernicious of all.

While in our room I looked to see what Emmie had been typing. Presumably it concerned the countess's biography, the details of which promised to be invigorating. Unfortunately, she'd removed whatever it was from the typewriter and the drawer of the table was locked.

I returned to find Lacy making a list of suspects on the slate. Kirsch held the top position. Then came Thomas, then Geneviève, and then the cook.

"Have you met the cook, Mr. Reese?"

"Well, inasmuch as I'm going to. A Frenchman. He speaks no English and isn't what you would call a friendly sort. His name is Gustave."

I chose not to mention his past employment at the German Embassy. I wasn't sure if Lacy knew the circumstances surrounding the prior count's death, but I saw no need to give him the rope to hang the fellow.

"All four foreigners," he said. "Interesting, isn't it?"

"Yes, though not so much in Washington, I imagine."

"Next is Captain Dumont." He wrote the name on the slate and then underlined it. "Another foreigner, who found it convenient to travel home *the very morning* the murder was discovered. Yes, I know, the *countess* says his departure had been planned. But even if that's true, it

26

would only mean that last night was an opportune time for executing an enemy. Yes, we must have a word with Captain Dumont. When I return to the office, I'll wire New York and see that he's stopped."

"He'll be traveling on a diplomatic passport." I wasn't comfortable mentioning the alibi the countess had so casually provided the Frenchman.

"I suppose he will. Nevertheless, I think my chief would consider it amiss if... I don't see you taking any notes, Mr. Reese."

"Yes, of course." I took pencil to notebook and repeated the action whenever there was a pause in the conversation.

Lacy turned back to the slate. "Next, I'm afraid, is Mrs. Reese. I expect she came down with you yesterday."

"Actually, two weeks ago."

"So! She would have had time to become acquainted with the count."

"Well, yes. But I can vouch for her. She was in bed when the lights went off."

"You had a light on?"

"She was reading."

"And you? Asleep?"

"Thinking."

"Ah, thinking. And being acquainted with Mrs. Reese, I can imagine *what* you were thinking. I remember you told me before, a most accommodating girl, your missus. But then that was five years ago. Would you say the same today, Mr. Reese?"

"Not in those exact words."

He chuckled. A change of subject seemed in order. I didn't like the sergeant examining my thoughts vis à vis Emmie while the two of us were lying in bed.

"Did I mention Captain Dumont is an officer of engineers?"

"No, Mr. Reese, you did not. Just the sort to invent a machine like that used to murder the count. Yes, just the sort...."

"Does that mean he goes to the top of the list?"

"No, I still say that valet is our best bet. But of course the list is not complete."

"You mean the countess?"

"The countess? No, let's set her aside for now."

"Probably wise. Not the little girl?"

"No, I think we can forget the little girl. I'm speaking of you, Mr. Reese. You arrive at a house where your wife has been spending time with a licentious aristocrat. A man, I think you'd agree, most women would find quite attractive."

"Of course, she can vouch for me as well."

"No doubt she could. Who's to say otherwise? But can you be sure she wouldn't feel disposed to bend the truth if she thought you were behind the cruel murder of her lover?"

The sergeant had a knack for formulating sentences that would have a Greek logician scratching his head. "You mean, if she thought I had killed the count, she might be disinclined to testify that I'd been in bed at the moment he was killed, even though I had been?"

"*Or* vice versa."

I decided to let the vice versa go by. The possible implications seemed too alarming to explore. "I suppose that would make sense, if we assume the device had been engineered by someone who knew that a third person would be visiting the count."

"Exactly, Mr. Reese. The actual killer would then be

free to establish an alibi for himself. But not only did he know the count would have a visitor, he also knew that this visitor would be entering via the door from the servants' hall. Now, let's work backward. Which of the eligible women would be likely to enter via the servants' hall?" He circled the name Geneviève. "All we need to do now is find out who in the house would have been angered to learn that the maid was having a tryst with the count. I noticed she has an eye for you, Mr. Reese."

"Mere friendliness. Besides, I only met her yesterday."

"Of course, it might not be *a man in love with the maid*. Perhaps a woman, another lover of the count's. According to the valet, he was the fickle sort. But first things first."

He pulled the bell cord and a short while later Geneviève appeared.

"Can I be of service?"

"Well, that's what we'd like to know."

"*Pardon?*"

"Sit down, Miss…"

"Lebeau."

"All right, Miss Lebeau. How long had you known the count?"

"He was already a guest here when I arrived."

"And when was that?"

"The first week of November."

"What happened to the maid before you?"

"Well, I believe she was dismissed, for some… *indiscrétion*."

"Oh! An indiscretion. And did this indiscretion involve the count?"

"I think, perhaps. I only know that the countess put

in a request with the agency, and they sent me. The countess found me satisfactory, so..." She gave a Gallic shrug.

"And what agency was that?"

"What agency? Mr. Chappelle's agency."

"Ah, Mr. Chappelle. Isn't that interesting?" he asked me rhetorically.

I had to agree with him on this, though for different reasons. I doubt you'll be surprised to learn I'd become well acquainted with Chappelle's employment agency during our last sojourn in Washington. (Yes, the coincidences are getting a bit thick. But surely the faithful reader appreciates the providential economizing of players.)

What made the Chappelle agency interesting in Lacy's eyes was that it had been owned by an educated negro whom he'd been unable to intimidate. That man had emigrated to France, and the agency was now owned by his brother, a fellow with a shady past and even more irksome to the sergeant.

But Lacy's fixation with the proper servility of the dark-skinned race had blinded him to what made the Chappelle agency truly noteworthy. It was, I had ultimately learned, a supplier both of servants and of information. The Chappelles maintained communication with the men and women they placed in the homes of Washington's politically powerful, ostensibly to ensure they provided satisfactory service. In fact, these maids, cooks, butlers, etc., acted as eyes and ears for the Chappelles' more lucrative line. What would a major railroad pay to know what Senator So-and-so has in mind with his modifications to the rate schedules? Or the sugar trust pay to learn of prospective changes to the tariffs?

This aspect of the Chappelle agency would have been well known to the countess—which made it curious she'd chosen that office to supply a new maid.

Lacy had moved on, grilling the maid about the count. So far, she had only agreed he was a very handsome man.

"And did you ever visit him? At night?"

"You're joking, *monsieur*. I just told you about the girl before me."

"And yet we know someone entered the room late last night, *from the servants' hall*."

"But the servants' hall also connects to the main hall upstairs, and..."

"And?"

"Well... there is also a door that leads to the countess's room." She looked down at her lap and nervously ran her hands along her apron.

"I see...." Lacy looked almost as anxious. "And the room shared by Mr. Reese and his missus?"

"No, that is on the side. Just the two larger bedchambers."

"I've one more question for you. Are you seeing any of the other servants?"

"*Seeing?*"

"You know what I mean. Taken in a show with Herr Kirsch, perhaps?"

"*Him?*" She made a noise that would have done nothing toward improving the valet's self-esteem.

"Or the cook? A fellow Frenchman, I understand."

She pursed her lips and nodded equivocally. "Sometimes... we..."

"Ah. That's all I needed to know."

"I may go?"

"For now. But send in this cook. I've some questions."

"Yes, but he speaks no English."

"Send him in just the same." She went out and he turned to me. "How's your French, Mr. Reese?"

"Rough. Maybe we should have Geneviève in with him to translate."

"Oh, that would be a fine idea, wouldn't it?"

"Well, I could fetch my wife, or the countess...."

"Let's not bother the countess. Mrs. Reese will do just fine."

I could hear the clatter from the front hall: Emmie was once again at work. This time when I entered, she looked over her shoulder at me, then quickly pulled whatever it was out of the typewriter. She put it in the drawer and rose.

"The countess's secrets revealed?"

"Yes... but not yet.... Solved the murder?"

"I have my suspicions."

"Have you shared them with Sergeant Lacy?"

"Should I?"

"Why ask me?"

"No reason. He wondered if you might be free to do some translation. He wants to interview the cook."

"The cook?"

"It seems he and Geneviève may have something going on. The sergeant suspects she might be the one who'd planned a liaison with the count last night."

"And the cook killed the count out of jealousy?"

"Just a theory."

I opened the door for her and she was nearly in the hall when she raced back and locked the drawer.

In the billiard room, Lacy hovered menacingly over the seated cook.

"All I can get from him is a lot of insolent looks."

"Perhaps I can help," Emmie suggested. "What would you like to ask him?"

"Ask him about his relationship with this Geneviève."

"*Monsieur, ce flic imbécile veut savoir quels sont vos sentiments pour la bonne, Geneviève.*"

"*Evidement, elle est très jolie, n'est-ce pas?*"

"He says he can't keep her out of his mind. He lies awake at night thinking of her. His work suffers, he squanders his money buying her gifts.... But still, she's indifferent."

"Said all that, did he?"

"You must remember, Sergeant, French is the language of love."

"Yes, we all know about the French. Ask him if he suspected the count might be having better luck with the girl."

"*Il demande ce-que le comte préférait manger au petit déjeuner.*"

"*Le comte? Mais je crois qu'il ne se levait jamais assez tôt pour le manger. Geneviève lui apportait du café et des croissants environ onze heures.*"

"*Combien de croissants?*"

"*Je ne sais pas—peut-être deux, ou trois s'il y en avait assez.*"

"He says often at night he hears Geneviève leave her room, up on the third floor, then come back an hour later. Sometimes twice in one night. Or even three times...."

"Sounds like a lot of going up and down stairs. How's he explain that?"

"*Il demande si Geneviève aime les croissants.*"

"*Geneviève? Bah! Comme cette fille-là bouffe.... Je suis étonné qu'elle ne soit pas devenue une fille grosse.*"

"He says the girl is insatiable. It amazes him she isn't... Well... In the pudding club...."

"In the pudding club?"

"An English colloquialism," Emmie explained. "It means with child."

"An insatiable girl who hasn't time for him? And him a Frenchman? I think we may have solved our case, Mr. Reese."

"I suppose it does look bad for the fellow. But could he have come up with that method?"

Just then, Geneviève entered.

"The carpenter is on the telephone. Gustave wanted to set a time for him to come by and fix the dumbwaiter." She then repeated the news to Gustave in French.

The cook rose and looked at Lacy.

"All right, run along. I think we learned all we need to from you."

"I should go, too," Emmie said.

"No, Mrs. Reese, you stay, if you don't mind. I have a few questions for you."

The two servants left us and Lacy closed the door. "Sit down please, Mrs. Reese."

"All right, if you think I can be of help."

"Tell me, what were your own feelings toward the late count?"

"Well, he was a strikingly handsome man. Very fit."

"Yes, he must have been.... But did you find yourself at all..."

"Attracted to him? Well," she looked over at me, "I'd be lying if I denied it. It wasn't simply his physique. He was also a very cultured man. You could discuss literature with him and not have to explain who Émile Zola is."

"And who is this Émile Zola?"

"Was. A renowned French novelist. I'm surprised a cosmopolitan like yourself isn't familiar with him."

"Well, like Mr. Holmes, I don't fill my brain with subjects unimportant to the work of a detective. That includes literature, astronomy, philosophy, chemistry...."

"I thought Holmes was something of an expert chemist," I said. "Wasn't he doing some experiment analyzing blood stains when Watson met him?"

"Indeed, that's true. But I have refined his doctrine."

"Ah. So you've taken the calculated ignorance to a higher level. Do you bother with the violin?"

"No, but I do sometimes play a hand or two of whist with the wife. A game Holmes himself never mastered. But getting back to our murder. Your husband tells me you were both in bed when the lights went out. Is that how you remember things?"

"Oh, yes. I was reading and he was asleep."

"Asleep, was he? Can you be sure?"

"Can I be sure? Well, he was snoring."

"One last question, Mrs. Reese. Did you ever visit the count in his room?"

"Not that I recall."

"Not that you recall? Perhaps if your husband were to leave the room your memory would improve."

"No, I never visited him in his room. Nor did he visit mine. I admit I found the count attractive, but really, Sergeant...."

"No cause to get annoyed, Mrs. Reese. I just need to check on all the suspects."

"Including the countess?"

"Are you implying she and the count..."

"I'm not implying anything. It's you who are making these wild conjectures. I think I had better go." She rose and walked to the door.

"All right, Mrs. Reese. But on your way, ask that Thomas to come in."

As the door closed, he turned to me.

"Are you at all worried about what might have gone on before your arrival, Mr. Reese?"

"With the count? Oh, no. Not at all."

I don't think he was persuaded. But he thankfully dropped the topic when he espied an uneaten pickle wedge on the one plate Geneviève had neglected to clear.

4

So far, I hadn't been especially forthcoming with the sergeant. I hadn't mentioned the countess's vouching for the whereabouts of Captain Dumont at the time of the murder. And I misled him when I said I was sure Emmie had been in bed when the lights went out. Most damningly, I hadn't mentioned the inciting scent I'd encountered in the hall, nor the certain bit of female anatomy which had accompanied it.

But in stating that I hadn't been worried about Emmie having a tryst with the count, I'd been entirely candid. My anxieties on that score lay elsewhere: Captain Dumont. To explain why, I need to back up and fill in the details of what prompted my visit in the first place.

The murder trial Emmie had been covering had taken place in upstate New York, the tiny county seat of Herkimer. It was the infamous Gillette case, the Adirondack murderer. Gillette (no relation to the doctor—at least as far as I know) had taken a young woman out onto Big Moose Lake. There she had drowned. Ultimately, the jury decided she had drowned with his help.

Emmie returned to Brooklyn the first week of December to find a letter waiting. It was a summons from the countess, but one with which Emmie was eager to comply. The noble lady indicated she was finally ready to reveal her life story—the only proviso being that the account be written so as not to identify her. Emmie set off immediately for Washington. She left open her return date, but assured me it would be before Christmas.

A week or so later, I received the first of several letters postmarked this city. They were written in a careful, female hand. And they warned of an intrigue between Emmie and a French officer by the name of Dumont. The initial letter was rather vague in its allusions. But it made a clear suggestion that I come to Washington immediately.

I felt disinclined to do so for several reasons. First, I was working a case of fire insurance fraud right there in Brooklyn which promised to be both undemanding and lucrative. Second, the last time I rushed off to thwart an assignation of Emmie's, it turned out to be a false alarm (at least until the hotel in which we were staying burned to the ground).

My principal reservation, however, was a deep-seated fear of annoying the countess. She and I had gotten along amiably during our last trip, but only because I'd assiduously avoided crossing her in any possible way. Showing up without an invitation was likely to put me well to the outside of favor.

The second letter arrived just days after the first. This one was more explicit in its accusations. It also contained a billet-doux addressed to "Emily, *ma chérie*," and another in her hand addressed to "*Cher capitaine, mon capitaine.*" They were both in French, but my correspondent had helpfully provided translations. The third letter, arriving the next day, contained two more billets-doux, also helpfully translated. Things seemed to be heating up, but it wasn't until the fourth envelope arrived that I became truly worried. His prose had become markedly more specific in its suggestions, while hers included certain locutions I couldn't recall Emmie using at home. The image inspired by "Aphrodite's rich drippings" is not one easily abandoned—especially when the stationery on which it is written sticks to one's fingers.

I sent Emmie a wire and asked if I should join her. Certainly not, was her reply. She also hinted she might not make it back for Christmas. The next morning, I received the fifth and final letter from my informer. It was brief: "The writing of love notes is over...."

An hour later, I was on a train to Washington. When I arrived that evening, Emmie was out. The countess greeted me coolly and summoned me to her study.

"You had better have a very good explanation, Harry."

"I've reason to believe Emmie has entered into a liaison with a French officer."

"Captain Dumont?"

"You know him?"

"Of course I know him, he's a guest in my home. And your aspersion is complete nonsense. Go back to Brooklyn before you make an ass of yourself—or worse."

"Well, then how do you explain this?" I handed her the sauciest of Dumont's love letters to Emmie.

She laughed. "I think I can guess who sent you this."

"Who?"

"Never mind who. Someone is having you on, though why I can't say."

"How can you be sure?"

She unlocked the top drawer of her desk and retrieved a letter, then handed it to me along with the one I'd just given her. They were nearly identical. The only difference I could glean was the salutation.

"But what does that prove except that this Captain Dumont is a bounder, and not even a particularly imaginative one?"

"You really are a naïf, Harry, aren't you? Do you honestly think a French officer would be so gauche as to send the same love letter to two women? Or so reckless? Yours is a forgery. I have the original."

"How can you be sure which..."

"Before you finish that thought, Harry, I suggest you think long and hard about whether you really want to push me into revealing details of my private affairs. Is my word not enough?"

"Of course, I didn't mean to imply..."

"Good. You may stay as my guest, Harry—as long as your wife doesn't object. But do be careful, won't you? Such a busy time of year—I've little patience for any sort of nuisance. Now you may go."

I left her and went to the room I'd be sharing with Emmie. There was Sesbania, going through my things. By the end of that reunion, I'd made two separate contributions to Mrs. Bradley's defense fund and had a very good idea who had forged the letters. She was five years older than the last time I saw her and she hadn't spent the time idly.

Thomas entered the billiard room. "Mrs. Reese tells me you wish to see me."

"That's right," Lacy told him. "Have a seat, Mr...."

"Uhl, U–H–L. Thomas Uhl. I would be more comfortable standing."

"Suit yourself. Uhl. Odd name, isn't it?"

"Not where I am from."

"Where's that?"

"Bavaria. I was brought over as a coachman, for the embassy."

"Then how did you end up as the butler here?"

"I was of service to the countess. When the count—

the previous count—her husband...When he... died unexpectedly, she asked me to join her staff here."

"So you were of service to the countess.... Interesting. Tell me, Thomas, what were your feelings toward the count?"

"Eh, which count?"

"The one who died upstairs."

"It isn't for a servant to have feelings toward a guest of his mistress."

"Oh, come now, Thomas. The man's been murdered."

"Well, if it will go no further. I thought him too careless with the affections of the ladies."

"Any lady in particular?"

"I... *To answer that is out of the question.*"

"Geneviève, I assume, was one. A very busy girl, from what I hear."

"Geneviève? I would never have allowed that."

"Oh? You have feelings for her yourself?"

"Of course not! But I am in charge of the staff, and responsible for their behavior."

"Well, how about Mrs. Reese? Oh, you may pretend Mr. Reese isn't here."

"Mrs. Reese? I know nothing about her affairs."

"*Affairs?*"

"I mean, I know nothing of what she..."

"Never mind. All right, Thomas. I can see I'll get nothing useful out of you. You may go."

Apparently, the sergeant had decided Thomas was too close to the countess to be pressed.

He took out his watch. "Past four. I'll need to head downtown if I'm going to have my chief send that wire to New York. We can begin again in the morning. What sort of arrangements are there for breakfast? My wife's gone to see her mother in Philadelphia, so nothing's to stop us from beginning first thing."

"Very casual—and plentiful. I'll head out with you. I need to do a little Christmas shopping—provided I can find my overcoat."

I'd assumed Lacy would be hiring a cab, but when we got out to Connecticut Avenue we played a little game, each expecting the other to hail one. When it was obvious neither of us would bite, we hopped on a crowded street car.

"To tell the truth, I prefer riding the cars," he told me. "Gives me a chance to observe."

His avowal would have been more convincing if the two of us weren't hanging on for dear life at the edge of the open platform. It must have been about fifteen degrees and there was a steady breeze coming down the avenue. Odds were, Sergeant Lacy had a stack of cab receipts and would be putting in for compensation and pocketing the difference.

When the car stopped beside a department store on F Street, I said good-bye and hopped off.

The store was filled to bursting and the crowd intoxicated with the Christmas spirit—all merry smiles and sharp elbows. It cost me twenty minutes and a bruised rib just to get to the perfume counter, and then another twenty minutes to be waited on. But I was a man with a mission. I'd decided I liked the mystery woman's choice of scent and thought perhaps Emmie would be amenable to it.

"I'm trying to locate this particular perfume," I told the salesgirl while handing over the book.

She took a sniff. "Oh... That is..." Then she took a

more thorough inhalation. "My, quite…"

"Inciting?"

"Oh! Well…" She blushed. "But I'm afraid I don't recognize it. Let me ask Mr. Jacobs."

She went off with the book and returned with a pompous-looking floor manager.

"It's right here on your book!" he told me.

"Yes, I was hoping you could identify it so I could purchase some."

"I mean the subtitle of the book, *Deux nuits d'excès*. That's what the perfume is called. I wondered where the name came from."

"How much does it run?"

"Oh, quite expensive—*if* you can get it."

"You don't have any?"

"No one in town can get it. I hear it can't even be had in New York. The only reason I'm familiar with it is that a Frenchwoman residing here requested it. All she had was the name and a letter bearing the scent. Our buyer is looking into having it shipped direct from Paris. In the meantime, maybe we can interest you in something else?"

"Too risky."

"Pardon?"

"No, thanks." I reached for the book.

"Just let me jot down the title. I'm sure our book department will want to stock it."

He handed back the book and I fought my way out to the street. Only, this time I wasn't so timid about it— you can't live in Brooklyn without learning a thing or two about the Christmas spirit.

This news concerning the scarcity of her scent only heightened my interest in the mystery woman. Someone must have thought very highly of her. My curiosity was provoked. I penciled in the rest of her based on my limited exploration of her anatomy, and, I must confess, she was stunningly attractive. There was also, of course, the small matter of the count's murder, which she may well have had a hand in. Duty obliged me to locate this fascinating female.

I had just three clues to her identity: her scent, her script, and her bookseller. I hadn't noticed it previously, but there was a plate inside the back cover for C.C. Pursell's shop on 9th Street, just a few blocks away. It too was packed with shoppers and I had to jostle several dozen out of the way just to get to the counter. Fortunately, bookworms are by and large slow-moving, docile creatures.

"I need some help finding someone," I told the man there. "You see, I was on a crowded car just now and the woman beside me left this book behind. I see from the plate that she bought it here and I'm wondering if you could give me her name so I can return it?" I handed him the book.

"*Gamiani!*" he said excitedly, then repeated it in a whisper. He wiggled a finger at me and drew me into a little office.

"We don't normally..."

"Of course, but how else can I find her?"

"Yes, but a book like this.... The lady had assumed our discretion. And we hers. I can't believe Miss Walker pasted a plate in it. I'll tell you what, leave it here and we will see it is returned to the lady in question."

"You've sold just one copy?"

"A special order, for a loyal client. It's certainly not something we stock."

My interest in the mystery woman was growing. I decided to play my trump card.

"I suppose if I were to show this to my colleague, Detective Sergeant Lacy, he might be able to persuade you to be a little more forthcoming."

"I see no reason to involve the police."

"Good. Neither do I. Give me her name, and I assure you it will go no further."

"All right. Mrs. Quinlan purchased it, the senator's wife." He gave me an address in Georgetown. "There is one thing."

"What's that?"

"Well, it's a delicate matter, but you see, it hasn't been paid for. I was reluctant to send a bill... in case..."

"In case her husband saw it?"

"Well, yes."

"What's the damage?"

"Eight dollars."

"*Eight dollars!* For this little tome?"

"If you knew how difficult it was to get a copy.... I'm sure Mrs. Quinlan will make you whole when you see her."

I paid him, but when he refused to give me a receipt by which I might be reimbursed, I put on my most indignant face and stomped out. It was the slow-moving bookworms who bore the brunt of it.

Wasting no time, I boarded another overcrowded car, this one bound for Georgetown. By the time I found the house on 31st Street, night had descended and a light snow was falling. As I drew near, a couple appeared on the porch—an older fellow I assumed to be the senator, and his much younger wife.

"I'll see what's holding up the carriage," he told her.

He walked by without seeming to notice me and entered an alley. I approached the lady. She was certainly attractive, but not so stunning as the figure I'd penciled in earlier.

"Mrs. Quinlan? I'm Harry Reese—a guest of the Countess von Schnurrenberger."

"Oh. I... I heard of the death of the count. She must be very upset."

"Not terribly, no. But what I want to tell you is this: someone visiting the count late last night seems to have sprung a trap. By opening a specific door, this person, probably unbeknownst to her, set in motion a device which brought about the count's electrocution."

Her mouth fell open and her eyes seemed to be trying to escape her skull. I sensed the news came as a surprise.

"How did you..."

"I came across the book the count was reading when he died."

"The book?" She turned from me toward a carriage just emerging from the alley. "I can't talk now. Come by tomorrow evening. Say, ten o'clock. Now go, please!"

I did as she asked, walking down to P Street, then across the bridge toward Dupont Circle. It was a short stroll from there to the countess's.

I went upstairs to find Emmie. As I passed her study, the countess beckoned to me through the open door. She was dressed in a stylish evening gown.

"I've been waiting for you, Harry. Close the door."

"Waiting for me?"

"Yes, I want to know what that little snoop has found out."

"Sergeant Lacy? Well, he *thinks* he's found out that

Geneviève was making regular visits to the count's chamber. And that Gustave was insanely jealous over that."

"What nonsense."

"Yes, well, we learned this via Emmie's efforts as translator. I suspected she was having a little fun."

"Anything else?"

"Only that Emmie found the count attractive, but insists she never visited him. Or he her."

"Stop scrutinizing me like that. Are you expecting me to betray some secret of Emmie's?"

"I only hoped... Oh, there is one more thing. Lacy was going to ask his chief to wire New York and have Captain Dumont picked up."

"Well, then it's a very good thing he sailed from Baltimore three hours ago."

"From Baltimore?"

"Yes, on a tramp steamer headed to Brest. He wired from the pier. It's far too late for the police to stop him now. Anything else?"

"No, I'd say Lacy is otherwise in the dark. Just as you wanted."

"Lacy is. But what about you?"

"Me? I'm not sure what you mean."

"Don't put on that dumb act with me, Harry. Surely you must be capable of some conjectures of your own."

"Well, I thought it might be safer to try to keep a lid on my conjectures."

"Yes. No doubt it would. Just remember that. Now I need to go. I'm late already."

"A Christmas party?"

"Ostensibly, but one celebrating the defeat of a railway bill as much as the birth of our Lord."

"Well, then *Onward Christian Soldiers*—with stops at Baltimore, Wilmington, Philadelphia, Trenton, and Newark Market Street Station."

The countess gave me a puzzled look, then shook her head and rushed off. I came upon Emmie as she exited our room.

"You don't need to change—it's just the two of us for dinner, though Sesbania may make an appearance."

The girl normally ate earlier, in the kitchen with the domestic staff. Presumably because of the late start to evening meals in the dining room. But I assumed it was also so she could listen in on the servants' conversation for her mentor.

I told Emmie all that had gone on with Lacy which she hadn't been privy to. In regard to her translations, she would only concede they were not literal.

"I thought I heard the word *croissant* in your exchanges with the cook. Yet you didn't mention them to Lacy."

"Oh.... A French idiom."

"Meaning?"

"A vulgarism too embarrassing to mention."

She then asked me several pointed questions about my whereabouts that evening. I deflected them with vague hints of having gone shopping.

It was after ten when we finished our dessert and went upstairs. Sesbania hadn't made an appearance, so I took it for granted she'd been spying on us from some secret nook.

5

No sooner had I gotten Emmie under the sheets than she reconvened the inquisition. She insisted on knowing where I'd done my shopping. I was equally determined, but she caught me off guard when she mentioned C.C. Pursell, bookseller.

"You followed me there?"

"Of course not. I was there on a similar mission. Listen, why don't we just exchange presents now?"

"Exchange presents?"

"All right. I'll go first...." She got up and took a wrapped package from the desk. "Merry Christmas, Harry." She handed it to me and gave me a peck on the cheek.

"Are you sure you want to? I haven't even had time to wrap yours. I..."

"You should have let them do it at the bookshop.... But it doesn't matter."

"I really think we should wait."

"*Harry,* I *heard* the clerk when you inquired about the book!" Then smiling, she whispered, "And I saw him take you into the office so as not to be seen with it...."

"Not to be seen with it?"

"*Gamiani!* Frankly, I'm amazed they stock a book like that at all. And that you would have remembered it."

"Remembered it?"

"In my book, Mrs. Biddle gives it to the girl she is trying to interest in languages. So gripping does the girl find it, she wears out a French dictionary in a single night. Don't pretend that isn't where you heard of it. I've never had a chance to read it myself. I only knew of it by reputation. It's considered one of the classics of erotic literature. Now hand it over, Harry. I've been patient long enough."

I went over and took the little book out of my jacket pocket. She grabbed it as soon as I was in range.

"*In anticipation*. Who wrote the inscription for you? The countess?"

"Ah... yes. I saw her just before she went out."

"The scent..." She sniffed the book. "Hmm. Now I know where you went after the bookshop."

"Do you? Where?"

"To a perfume counter. Oh, Harry, you know I don't wear scent."

"Yes... I remembered that after testing one or two. So I bought the book instead."

"You have it backwards. You must have taken the book to the perfume counter." She sniffed it again. "You know, if I *did* wear scent... What's it called?"

"Eh... Don't recall."

"Oh, well." She set down the book. "Now you open your present."

It was a nicely bound three-volume set of Conan Doyle's Sherlock Holmes stories.

"I thought it might help you to brush up, given Sergeant Lacy's admiration for Holmes."

"Yes, thank you, Emmie. It's very timely. He's enlisted me as his Dr. Watson and I could use some literary pointers." I leaned over to kiss her, but she was already lost in her book.

I opened up the first volume to *The Sign of Four*, a novella I'd read previously and which had come to mind earlier that day. The policeman Holmes humbles in this episode is Mr. Athelney Jones, described by Watson as a portly man who strides heavily and has small, twinkling eyes and a florid, puffy countenance. He speaks in a playful, usually sarcastic, manner and maintains a general disdain for the opinions of others. Ironically, the very model for Detective Sergeant Lacy—though I somehow doubted he'd appreciate the irony were it brought to his attention.

Emmie was still reading when I nodded off. She'd been thoroughly engrossed, though every once in a while she would stop to smell the book. When last I saw her, her eyes had a mischievous cast, and her mouth hung slightly open. I suppose one has a right to expect such things from an eight-dollar book. I'd have to see if there was an English translation available.

She must have fallen asleep reading. On rising, I turned off her lamp and dressed in the semi-darkness of a December morning, then left the room as quietly as possible.

Lacy was already in the dining room when I arrived. He had a mounded plate before him, but was riveted by a sheet of paper he was reading. Sesbania stood just beside him. When she saw me approaching, she whispered sharply, "Quick!"

Lacy looked up, then hurriedly folded the paper and stuck it in an inside pocket of his jacket. He patted the girl on the head.

"The child's given me a poem she's written. I want to take it home and show the missus."

"Does it involve a wronged woman who guns down a man?"

"A little girl and her dolly," he said smiling.

Sesbania found the thought of such an ode as revolting as I did. Her nose wrinkled, and she trotted out of the room. I made up a plate and had just sat down when Lacy asked if there was any orange marmalade available, as the lemon variety on the sideboard wasn't to his liking. I rang the bell, but after some time I poked my head into the kitchen, where Geneviève was in conference with a tradesman.

"Mr. Reese, this is Mr. Dunlap—he came about the dumbwaiter. I'm not sure what he is telling me."

"It's simple enough," the man told me. "Someone's taken the pulleys from the thing. I thought they came loose and fell to the bottom of the shaft, but I opened it up and they ain't there."

"Ah. Say, four pulleys, about yea big?"

"Yeah. You seen 'em?"

"Yes, I believe I may have." I led him up the back stairs and into the count's bedroom. "There, on the back of the bureau."

"That's them, all right. But what are they doing on the dresser?"

"A murder weapon, of a sort." I explained how the thing worked, but his enthusiastic admiration for the design caused me to regret my decision. Jealous lovers are everywhere and I feared I'd soon be reading about the electrocution of his wife's paramour, or the husband of *his* paramour.

I reported the matter to Lacy when I returned, but he was more concerned with the limited selection of jam.

"Oh. No orange marmalade, I'm afraid," I said, with as much sympathy as I could muster. "I wonder if this new information doesn't militate against Gustave as the engineer of the contraption?"

"I don't see that at all, Mr. Reese. No orange marmalade, in a house like this?"

"Well, suppose Gustave *had* set it up. Once the count had been electrocuted, he could have gone back to the room and disassembled the thing, put the pulleys back in the dumbwaiter, and we'd never have been the wiser. Same for the valet, or Thomas."

"But why not Captain Dumont as well? Or you yourself, for that matter? You've eliminated all the suspects."

"Yes. Unless the engineer was indisposed at the time...."

"Ah. In the company of a lover. I would be careful, Mr. Reese. If anything, you've pointed a finger at yourself!"

"Have I?"

"Suppose you came here suspecting your wife was interested in meeting the count. You arrive, and soon conclude she visits him in his room. You must be familiar with all sorts of mechanical devices in your work. Maybe you even formulated your plan before you left Brooklyn."

"I don't see how I could have planned the thing without knowing the house or the habits of the count."

"You've not been in the house before?"

"Well, yes. But years ago. Before this count had inherited the job."

"Then suppose you had an ally in the house?"

"If I do, they're keeping pretty quiet about it."

"Now suppose at some point your first evening here, you sneak into the servants' hall, disassemble the dumbwaiter, set up the machine behind the bureau, saw the table leg, and make your way out. Later, when your wife thinks you're asleep, she creeps off for her assignation. In case she's noticed, she goes down through the kitchen and up the back stairs. She opens the servants' door. The count is electrocuted. She hurries back to your room. You are awake, and voice some suspicion. To take your mind off that, she becomes friendly, if you know what I mean, exhibiting an unusual willingness to—well, we needn't go into that. Perhaps you intended to return to the count's room to remove the evidence of your crime, but she has distracted you. Now, what do you think of *that* as a working theory, Mr. Reese?"

"I can't say I'm particularly fond of it." I was surprised he'd come up with something so plausible—at least until the point where Emmie exhibits the unusual willingness in the wee hours of the morning.

"Don't worry, Mr. Reese. I wasn't accusing you." He laughed. "Only showing that we can't know why the killer didn't take the opportunity to remove his machine."

"Good morning." Emmie had entered the room without our noticing. "Already hard at work?"

"The sergeant was just making a case for me as the count's killer. While perhaps not so culpable, you played a rather energetic part."

"Killed him in a fit of jealousy?"

"Is there any reason for his being jealous?" Lacy asked.

"Well, Harry isn't always rational when it comes to his suspicions. I might mention a certain Pinkerton detective up in Maine whom Harry tortured on the mistaken assumption he and I were planning a tryst."

"Is that a fact, Mrs. Reese?" Lacy wasn't smiling now.

"Oh, yes. When we left town, the man was on crutches."

"On crutches?"

"A mere sprain," I assured him. "I interrogated the

man because he was acting suspiciously. You know how shifty those Pinkertons are."

"I do indeed. Still, the episode could shed some light on the present case."

"Has Dr. Watson ever been suspected by Mr. Holmes?" Emmie asked.

"That we will never know, Mrs. Reese. The good doctor is hardly likely to confide that bit of information, is he?"

"Very true. Tell me, Sergeant. How exactly did Harry wheedle himself into your confidence?"

"There's been no wheedling, Mrs. Reese. And besides, I'm not foolish enough to confide entirely in anyone. If you remember, Mr. Holmes almost always leaves Watson in the dark about some aspect of the case."

"True. And if Harry *is* guilty, keeping him close at hand is probably wise."

"Now you are thinking like a policeman, Mrs. Reese."

Geneviève came in with a fresh pot of coffee. As she turned to leave, Emmie stopped her.

"When you took the count his breakfast, was he usually still in bed?" she asked.

"*Oui.* He always read the morning newspaper in bed."

"What time was that?" Lacy asked.

"He usually rang about half past ten or eleven," she told him, then went back to the kitchen.

"Very interesting," Lacy said. "Very interesting, indeed."

"How so?" Emmie asked.

"It's simple, Mrs. Reese. If the killer knew that the maid would enter while the count was still in bed, *and*

55

reading, he didn't need to depend on there being a lady visitor during the night. It's looking very bad for that cook."

"How do you mean?"

"The girl would have told him how the count read in bed in the morning, just ordinary kitchen gossip. And perhaps she didn't always return as promptly as she might have.... If you know what I mean."

"Oh!" Emmie ejaculated.

She most certainly was up to something.

"Finish up, Mr. Reese. We must make preparations. Good day, Mrs. Reese."

He toddled off to the billiard room.

"What was that all about?" I asked her.

"I just remembered the count breakfasted in his room."

"Uh-huh." I finished my eggs and wiped my face, then went over and gave her a peck on the cheek. "Good-bye, dear. I must be off and undo your frame-up of the cook."

"I don't know what you're talking about, Harry."

"Hmm." I was nearly in the hall when she called after me.

"Harry. That perfume... I think it would be fun to try it."

"Eh... Remember, I got you the book instead."

"Yes, but..." Her voice took a turn to the coercive: "You still haven't seen my new negligee...."

"Good morning!" Sesbania was at the sideboard pouring herself some juice.

I hadn't noticed her come in. And I felt reasonably sure Emmie hadn't either. She was busily sopping up spilt coffee when I left.

Lacy had erased the roll of suspects from the slate and was constructing a new list.

"It's obvious now who committed the crime," he told me. "The cook had the motive, and the opportunity."

"Perhaps, but so might just about everyone else in the house."

"Oh, come, Mr. Reese. Do you honestly think your wife could disassemble a dumbwaiter and construct that device in the bedroom?"

"Not without detailed instructions."

"Or the countess?"

"Well…" I almost let slip something about master jewel thieves having surprising talents. Fortunately, my unerring sense of self-preservation prevailed. "No, that would seem unlikely. But I did learn something which puts Captain Dumont in rather a bad light."

"And you haven't mentioned it?"

"Only learned of it last evening. It seems he didn't go to New York with plans to sail today. He caught a tramp steamer out of Baltimore yesterday afternoon. Must be hundreds of miles out by now."

"Who told you this?"

"The countess. I suppose you could call her in to confirm it."

"No. That won't be necessary. There's no reason to think she lied about it."

Except, of course, that it refuted what she'd already said about Captain Dumont's exit being planned in advance.

"If he *did* leave in a hurry," the sergeant went on, "there may be something left in his room. Do you know where he slept?"

"Yes, in the room just past ours."

The countess had come down for breakfast and was once more in conference with Emmie and Sesbania when we passed through the hall. They went quiet on seeing us, all three looking their most inscrutable.

Dumont's room was larger than ours, but not nearly so large as the count's. Perhaps a matter of social rank, or a sign of who was most in the countess's favor.

The bureau and wardrobe were empty. But his trunk was still there, all tied up, with a Paris address affixed.

"Well, well. What have we here? A bit of luck. Must be waiting for an opportune moment for shipping it off."

He copied the address, then took out a pocket knife and cut the ropes. There was a dress uniform on top, complete with sword and brass-and-leather helmet. Then a pile of light summer wear, a large stack of books, three boxes of Cuban cigars, a bronze plate apparently pried off the U.S. Department of War, and, beneath all that, a leather rucksack containing a rather extensive collection of ladies' undergarments: garters, negligees, stockings, and a few intriguing items I wasn't myself able to identify.

I moved everything carefully to the bed, where we examined it—save one of the more intriguing items which I stuck in a pocket. I thought I might use it as a gift for Emmie, in lieu of the perfume I knew to be unobtainable.

When we had finished, Lacy took out a little tape measure and knelt down beside the trunk. "Just as I suspected...."

"Ah. A false bottom?" It's remarkable how useful the habit of reading detective novels is for a protagonist.

"Yes, exactly, Mr. Reese. Now we are getting someplace."

He felt around the inside, then used his knife to pop out the thin sheet of wood that purported to be the bottom. Below it were a number of separate compartments. Four were taken up with a not insubstantial amount of U.S. currency, several thousand dollars, I estimated, all in twenty-dollar bills. The other compartments contained bundles of what looked like personal correspondence. Most of them scented—none familiarly.

Lacy began flipping through each stack. "All in French.... Ah, what have we here? One with no post-mark.... Well, well... Your missus, Mr. Reese, her name's Emily, isn't it?"

"What's that?" I took the letter he offered me. It was Emmie's handwriting all right. It seemed that the countess had for some reason covered up for her.

"I think we could stand to use a different translator this time, Mr. Reese. Don't you?"

"Yes. I suppose we had better." I wasn't keen on Lacy learning the details of Emmie's interactions with Dumont—but I was very keen on learning them myself.

"Go and fetch that maid."

I went out into the hall and heard Emmie typing in our room. The door of the countess's study was just barely ajar and I could see her lying on the sofa reading some correspondence. It must have been pretty steamy stuff because her moans and sighs alternated with some very telling oohs. I turned to see Sesbania approaching me on the stairs.

"Have you seen Geneviève?"

"Kitchen, doing dishes. Can I be of some help?"

"Ah... no, thanks."

I found Geneviève drying plates. She had enlisted Kirsch to perform the actual washing. He was wearing one of her aprons and diverting her with some anecdote in French. It must have been decidedly amusing because both Geneviève and Gustave, who was at his table rolling out dough, broke into repeated bouts of laughter. It didn't seem fair intruding on their fun, so I occupied myself by attempting to follow the story. Most of the action was lost on me, but two nouns with which I was acquainted occurred repeatedly: *mamelon* and *escargot*. How the snail related to the nipple was to remain a mystery; the only thing I felt confident of was that snails themselves are nippleless.

Geneviève told me she'd be happy to oblige. We took the back stairs up and entered the main hall. Emmie could still be heard typing. I led the maid to Dumont's former room, but Lacy was gone. I went and checked the bathroom, and then the count's room, but when I saw no sign of him, I let Geneviève get back to her dishes.

Soon after, I found the sergeant in the billiard room. He was laid out on the baize table with his hands folded neatly on his stomach.

6

There was a sinister—almost funereal—aspect to the scene and I felt genuine relief when I was at last able to find a pulse. I went out to the telephone and found Dr. Gillette's number listed in a little address book beside it.

"A police sergeant? ...Yes, I remember Lacy. ...I'm free now. As a matter of fact, I was hoping for an excuse to return. I seem to have left without my coat and hat.... The countess, is she...?"

"She's acclimated to the idea that the count was murdered."

"I see. Good. I'll be there shortly."

In the kitchen I explained about Lacy and asked for a damp cloth. Geneviève returned with me to the billiard room and ministered to the still-unconscious detective.

"Sergeant Lacy is under the impression Gustave is very fond of you," I told her.

"We get along very well."

"Fonder than that. Even jealous of the attentions of others."

"That's silly. The attentions of what others? Herr Kirsch?"

"He's thinking of the count."

"I *told* you," she said impatiently, "there was never the slightest indiscretion."

"What about flirtation?"

"Well, the count flirted with everyone! Even little Sesbania."

"Let's keep that to ourselves. But suppose Gustave

observed him flirting with you and leapt to the conclusion there was something more to it?"

"But why would he care? Gustave has more than enough to keep him busy already."

"His duties as cook preclude romantic attachments?"

"His duties as cook?" She laughed. "No, I mean Elsie, the maid two houses down. And the quiet governess, over on California Street. And the rich young widow up on Kalorama—he brings her pastries at midnight. She's the obsession of the moment." Her tone had shifted by the final sentence of her account.

The doorbell rang and I went out to the hall. Thomas was there letting in Dr. Gillette.

"Your patient is in the billiard room, through the parlor," I told him. "Do you know the way?"

"Yes, I've been there before."

He went off and I stopped Thomas.

"Sergeant Lacy was assaulted upstairs a little while ago. Did you happen to see, or hear, anything suspicious?"

"No, nothing unusual."

What ranked as usual in that house was anyone's guess.

"Where were you, say, twenty minutes ago?" I asked.

He paused before answering. "On a commission for the countess. A private matter."

"You mean, out of the house?"

"If you insist on knowing, I was attending the countess in her study. If you want further details, you will need to ask her."

"No, that's quite all right, thank you." Perhaps the

moaning and sighing I'd heard wasn't due entirely to her steamy correspondence.

Back in the billiard room, Geneviève was helping the doctor bandage Lacy's head.

"Just a bad contusion," he said. "I'm surprised it knocked him out. What hit him?"

"I was hoping you might venture a guess."

"Nothing sharp-edged. Maybe one of those cue sticks."

"It's likely the assault occurred upstairs. Then whoever did it brought him down here."

"Why?"

"No idea. I suppose anyone could have made the wound—a woman... even a child?"

Geneviève made a noise. She apparently lived under the delusion Sesbania was a normal little girl.

"A woman, certainly. A child, perhaps. But could either move him downstairs and onto the table? He must weigh well over 200 pounds."

"No, not alone."

At last, Lacy stirred. The prospect of having to inform the countess that the police sergeant investigating a murder in her home had been himself murdered was not one I had looked forward to eagerly. And not least because she was one of the more likely suspects in both cases.

I explained to the sergeant how I had found him. He had no memory of being knocked out, nor had he heard anyone enter the room where he'd been examining Captain Dumont's correspondence.

"I think you should go at once to a hospital," Gillette told him. "I see no sign of a concussion. But in cases such as this, it is advisable..."

"And give my molester time to cover his tracks? No, Doctor, there'll be no malingering in the hospital."

"As you wish," the doctor conceded. "Mr. Reese, may I have a word?"

We stepped out into the parlor.

"My coat and hat... I left in rather a hurry last time.... The servant who answered the door knew nothing about them...."

He was interrupted by the telltale jingle of a coin-laden tin can.

"Care to make a contribution?"

"My advice is to give generously," I whispered to him. "Only afterward inquire about your coat and hat."

Lacy was getting down off the table when I returned. Geneviève helped him to a chair, then left us alone.

"Someone didn't want me reading those letters, Mr. Reese."

I didn't like the way he was looking at me. "Don't you think the money might have been a pretty good lure?"

"Perhaps. Have you ascertained the inhabitants' whereabouts?"

"Well, both Gustave and Kirsch were in the kitchen with Geneviève. So they're out."

"And that Thomas?"

"Says he was with the countess in her study. I saw her there as I passed—the door was ajar. My wife was in our room typing. And Sesbania was coming upstairs as I went down."

A young uniformed policeman knocked and entered the room excitedly.

"What is it?" Lacy asked.

"I was sent to tell you about Dumont."

"What about him?"

"No trace of the Frenchman has been found in New York. And he isn't listed as a passenger on any boat leaving this week."

"Yes, yes. We know that. You can go on back."

The man started out, but Lacy stopped him. "Wait a minute. Go upstairs, last door on the left. There's a trunk in the room. Keep an eye on it." The underling went off to do as bidden and Lacy turned to me. "You should have thought of that, Mr. Reese. When you arrived back upstairs with the maid, the trunk was still there, open?"

"Yes, but I didn't examine it closely."

"The letters and money?"

"I saw some letters lying about, but don't remember seeing the money. When there was no sign of you, I went off looking."

"Leaving the girl alone with the trunk?"

"Only briefly. When I didn't see you upstairs, I let her go back to her duties. Then I came downstairs and that's when I found you in here, out cold."

"Well, think: why would someone bother carting me down here?"

"Ah. To be alone with the trunk."

The patrolman entered the room once again, even more excitedly than before.

"There *is* no trunk in the last room on the left."

"*What?*"

With an astonishing burst of energy, Lacy charged up the stairs. Just as his man had reported, the trunk was gone. Once we'd checked the other rooms upstairs, I peeked in the countess's study. She was at her desk writing. I nudged the door open wider and saw neither Thomas nor the trunk. She hadn't seemed to have noticed me, but without looking up from her letter, she indicated otherwise.

"Why in god's name are you spying on me, Harry?"

"We seem to have misplaced Captain Dumont's trunk."

"Well, it's not in here. Why all the excitement? Boots tramping up and down the stairs."

"While he was looking through the trunk, Sergeant Lacy was knocked unconscious."

"Oh, dear. Good-bye now, Harry.... And close the door."

The two policemen and I searched the remainder of the house thoroughly, but saw no sign of the trunk. Emmie and Sesbania, as well as Gustave, Kirsch, and Geneviève, denied having any knowledge of its whereabouts. Thomas appeared to be out of the house. Lacy posted the patrolman by the door to stop him the moment he returned.

"Well, Mr. Reese. A tough break, to be sure, but perhaps a stroke of luck for you."

"How so?"

"You looked my best suspect. You could very easily have crept back after leaving me with the trunk, knocked me out, carried me downstairs, and only *then* called on the maid."

"I suppose. But Sesbania saw me on my way down, empty-handed."

"Children are quite easily swayed, Mr. Reese."

I'd have liked to see him try it with that child.

"It's the disappearance of the trunk," he went on, "that muddies the water. I don't see how you would have had time—unless that maid... You two do seem rather chummy...."

I didn't like where this was going. Luckily, the sergeant was diverted when the patrolman brought Thomas into the billiard room.

"Where have you been, man?"

"On a private commission for the countess."

"A private commission? What can you tell us about that trunk in Captain Dumont's room?"

"Captain Dumont's trunk? The express company came for it while you were in conference here with the doctor."

"What express company?"

"I didn't hear the name. But they had Captain Dumont's order."

"Was the trunk open when you went up?" I asked.

"No, all tied up, just as I had left it."

"Left it when?" Lacy asked.

"The day before Captain Dumont departed."

Lacy looked at me in disgust, then turned back to Thomas. "Did anyone else see them come and go?"

"Not that I'm aware. The countess may have observed them."

"Didn't these express handlers leave a receipt?"

"I didn't think to ask for one."

"Oh, didn't you? Well, we'll be calling them all. There are only so many in town. And you better hope that trunk is intact."

"Of course it is intact."

"And the money? And the letters?"

"I know of no letters, or any money. Only items of apparel, and some souvenirs."

"Just what did this commission for the countess involve?" Lacy was eyeing the paper parcel in the servant's hand.

"Are you demanding to know the details of the countess's private affairs?"

"I'm demanding to know what you were out doing when the trunk was discovered to have vanished from the house."

The servant opened the package and displayed the little carton inside. "The countess sent me to the druggist for this." It was a laxative. "You may ask her about it, if you disbelieve me. Should I go and ask her to come down?"

"No, you needn't mention a thing to her. Now go on," Lacy told him, then sent the uniformed man to telephone the express companies.

"What a house! Have you ever seen anything like it, Mr. Reese?"

"No, I can't say I have. Certainly some strange goings-on. Are you operating on the theory that the two crimes are linked, the count's murder and the assault on you?"

"Linked almost certainly, but I've reason to believe they weren't committed by the same hand." He reached in the inside pocket of his jacket and pulled out the folded paper he'd been reading at breakfast. "Read this."

It was a letter from Dumont to the count threatening him with dismemberment if he didn't cease directing his attentions toward an unidentified woman of their common acquaintance. Two facets of the note struck me as odd. First, the description of the gruesome dismemberment was unnecessarily detailed. Three paragraphs devoted to the topic seemed one too many. Second, the letter had been written in English, the first language of neither correspondent, but the sole language readable by Sergeant Lacy.

I handed it back. "I suppose that closes the matter." I didn't for a moment believe it, but anything that deflected suspicion from myself was welcome.

"Dumont killed the count, no doubt. But over who?"

I shrugged. "An unnamed woman."

"Unnamed, but don't pretend the description is unknown to you. The languid eyes, the lubricious lips, and the button nose...."

He waited for a response, but I sensed danger in every direction.

"Your wife, man!"

"Ah. Well, the eyes I can explain. She was up late reading. And the lips, that's just something she rubs on to keep them from getting chapped. But I can't say her nose ever struck me as button-like."

"The point, Mr. Reese, no matter how hard you try to obscure it, is that the count was killed over your wife. And though his murderer has absconded, the motive remains. Which brings us back to the small matter of who bludgeoned me. Now, if Kirsch and the cook were both in the kitchen, they're out of the running."

Lacy seemed to be eyeing me prospectively again. "Of course, it's possible it was someone from outside the house," I suggested. "The doors here are only locked at night. Maybe someone knew about the money...."

"Who?"

"Someone who knew how Dumont came by it. Say, someone he gambled with."

"A bit far-fetched, Mr. Reese, but possible."

"More than just possible. Especially if this fellow felt Dumont had cheated him. He looked like the type who'd deal from a cold deck."

"Maybe there's something in that. *Maybe*."

His uniformed man gave a brief knock and entered.

"I think I found the company that took away the trunk. The only thing is, they had the address of the house next door."

"Idiots. Where is it now?"

"They took it to the French Embassy."

"The embassy! Now we'll never get a look at it.... All right, go on back downtown."

The patrolman left us and Lacy went back to eyeing me. "You know what I think, Mr. Reese?"

"I wouldn't want to venture a guess."

"Rather than an intruder sneaking into the house and knocking me out, it might be more probable it was someone who didn't want me reading those letters. Someone who didn't want his dirty laundry put out to view.... Now that problem's solved."

Thankfully, Geneviève chose just that moment to poke her head in the door and divulge the one piece of news sure to divert the detective. "Luncheon is served in the dining room, gentlemen."

"Well, this promises to be a meal," Lacy said while theatrically rubbing his hands.

We found the countess, Emmie, and Sesbania already seated and the table crowded with victuals: a large leg of lamb, broiled vegetables, gravy, biscuits, and beer in lieu of wine. It was all quite good, but also quite unlike the light fare at the previous midday meals. It reeked of ulterior motive.

"How is the case progressing, Sergeant?" the dowager asked. "I understand you suffered a fall this morning."

"Not a fall, Your Ladyship. Someone deliberately knocked me out."

"I'll bet an intruder," Sesbania opined.

"And what makes you think that, miss?"

"Well, just after I passed Mr. Reese as I was coming upstairs, I heard a noise. Like a window opening. I decided it must have come from the count's room. So I went into the servants' hall, and very quietly opened the door from there into the count's room. Just as I did so, someone closed the other door. I went over to the window and saw a ladder leaning against the house. I assumed Charlie was washing the outside of the windows, as that's one of his duties. And perhaps he just needed to use the bathroom. So I went down to the kitchen for some milk and forgot about it."

"Washes the windows when it's twenty degrees out?"

"Yes, that did seem curious. And something else as well. I found these on the floor, just inside the window, as if they'd fallen from a pocket when whoever it was came over the sill."

She went over to Lacy and placed a pair of dice on the table beside his plate.

"Well, well, Mr. Reese. Perhaps the theory of a gambler looking to recoup his losses isn't quite so unlikely as you thought. I suppose he might even have tied the trunk back up."

"And called the express company—to get rid of the evidence," Sesbania added.

"That solves that," Emmie said. "But still leaves the count's death to explain."

"Yes, we still have that." Lacy smiled at her, then when she looked away, he gave me a wink.

"I assume you've examined the count's correspondence," the countess said.

"It mostly involved some suits he was having made in New York," I told her. "And a few letters from Germany, from his lawyers, I think."

"Then you haven't found his *private* correspondence. I believe he kept it in a little casket. You didn't see it in his room?"

"I don't see how we could have missed it, Your Ladyship," Lacy told her.

"Well, just the same, I suggest you look again after lunch." Then she changed the subject. "I understand from Emmie that you are a protégé of Mr. Holmes, Sergeant."

"His methods work just as well on this side of the ocean, Your Ladyship."

"Leave off the Ladyship, please. Are you also an authority on obscure blends of tobacco? Things of that nature?"

"Well, as a matter of fact, just as Mr. Holmes examined various types of ash in his monograph, I have made my own examination, and prepared my own monograph."

"On the ash of American tobacco?"

"Eh, no, Your Ladyship, I mean, no, Missus... eh, no. Mine is of a different nature. More in line with American habits."

"I'm afraid I don't understand. What is your monograph about?"

"Expectoration, ma'am."

"You wrote a monograph on spittle?"

"Not just spittle—all types. And not just wrote—illustrated with photographs. Which is why I'm having a difficult time finding a publisher. They complain they wouldn't be able to recoup the expense of printing."

"With the popularity of that repulsive habit in this country? Publishers are all fools, Sergeant Lacy."

"I couldn't agree more, ma'am."

"Nor I," Emmie chimed. She'd had no shortage of frustrations herself with trying to find a publisher.

Immediately after dessert—a very tasty apple crumble, served with ladles of heavy cream—Lacy and I went up to the count's bedroom. There was indeed a ladder propped outside the window, just as Sesbania had reported. But when we had made our search for Captain Dumont's trunk, there most definitely was not. I'd gone out to the carriage house and remembered bumping into it where it hung on the wall.

Consequently, I wasn't at all surprised when we found a small wooden chest under the bed. In fact, I would have been shocked if we hadn't.

It was locked and the sergeant had me fetch the valet.

"Do you recognize this, Herr Kirsch?"

"Of course. It is where the count kept his more... confidential documents."

"Where was it when we searched the room the morning of his death?"

"Here, I feel certain. Not that I remember seeing it. My mind was, of course, on other matters."

"Yes, like covering your tracks. Where's the key?"

"The key? I had no need to know where the count kept the key. Perhaps it was in his nightclothes when he was taken away?"

"We'll see if it shows up on the coroner's report. In the meantime, we need something to pry it open with."

"You mean to read the count's intimate correspondence?"

"Yes, I do!"

"Perhaps this will help." It was Sesbania, appearing from nowhere and holding a fireplace poker.

"Yes, I believe it will, miss." Lacy went over and she handed it to him. "At least someone in this house knows how to make herself helpful."

"Almost prescient," I added. Sesbania gave me her most ingratiating smile, then skipped out of the room—surprisingly incurious about the count's intimate correspondence.

In the meantime, the sergeant had pried open the casket. There were several letters in a woman's hand. Lacy handed them to me. They were scented, but not incitingly, and in German, a language which I had studied in college. Unfortunately, that was more than ten years before. I got the general gist, recognizing several anatomical references—my linguistic forte. But it seemed doubtful these letters mailed from Europe months before had anything to do with the aristocrat's murder.

"Now this *is* interesting." He handed me a typewritten page. "What do you make of that, Mr. Reese?"

The sheet was covered with numbers—a long list, divided into "words" of from one to several digits separated by commas, and then into paragraphs.

"A code of some sort?"

"What do you know of this, Herr Kirsch? Was your master here as an agent for the German government? Or something more sinister?"

"I... I... I am certain the count was nothing of the sort." He was uncharacteristically nervous. "There must be some other explanation."

"Well, when you think of one, you come and tell me. Now, you can go."

He went out through the servants' door.

"A lot of new grist for the mill," I said. "I suppose this broadens the list of potential suspects."

"Indeed it does, Mr. Reese. Indeed it does."

I welcomed the reprieve, however dubious the justification.

7

Lacy and I returned to the billiard room with the coded page of numbers. We were in agreement that the next step was to systematically test these figures against the various ciphers known to exist until we found the one that fit—the problem being that neither of us was all that familiar with the various ciphers known to exist. In investigations of insurance fraud, one rarely comes across a subject foolish enough to make written plans, or so literarily inclined as to make use of a cipher.

I had, however, recently read an American edition of Gaboriau's immensely popular detective novel *Monsieur Lecoq*. In that book, M. Lecoq—a brilliant French predecessor of Sherlock Holmes—is confronted with a page of numbers very similar to ours. Almost at once, he determines that the criminal and his confederate are using the double-book cipher. The way it works, I explained to Sergeant Lacy, is that the person sending the message picks a page at random in a book the two have previously agreed upon. He records the page number and then counts words from the top of the page until he finds the word he wants. Then counts off from that word until he finds his second word, etc., recording each number in succession. The one receiving the message turns to the page indicated by the first number, then likewise counts off words until he deciphers the message.

"It's an unbreakable code—*unless* one knows the book the two are using," I concluded.

"How'd M. Lecoq get around that?" Lacy asked.

"Well, in his case the man in question was a prisoner and only had one book in his possession." Yes, a pretty feeble plot device, but in my business one learns to let that sort of thing go by.

"Our count, unfortunately, wasn't a prisoner."

"No, but his traveling library was limited. We just need to test the code against the books he had with him."

"Back upstairs? I'll tell you what, Mr. Reese, I'll leave that to you. Meanwhile, I'll stay down here and think things through. A lot has transpired today, and it's important I keep the threads untangled."

I returned to the count's room fairly certain my efforts would be rewarded.

There were more than a dozen books lined up along the back of the writing table. But one candidate stood out from the others. It had a distinctive tan cover with a red border, and was the only book in English. It was the Becky Sharp Edition of Thackeray's *Vanity Fair*, the special edition issued to commemorate Mrs. Fiske's production of the play, *Becky Sharp*, which had been staged in New York a year or so before Emmie and I were married.

Though not much of a reader myself, I was for three reasons familiar with this book. First, despite missing Mrs. Fiske's production, I had seen Weber & Fields' amusing burlesque of it. Second, the case in Buffalo where I first met Emmie involved a man who used names from Thackeray's book as pseudonyms for persons of his acquaintance. Third, that next Christmas Emmie had presented me with this identical book.

And when I say identical, I mean just that. Inside the front cover was the inscription *To Harry, Christmas 1900*. I had never gotten around to actually reading the book—Weber & Fields' effort having amply sated my appetite for Thackeray—so it may be that Emmie was under the impression I'd forgotten all about it. And I had. At least, until the day of her departure a fortnight or so before. I saw her remove it from the shelf, doubtless to read on the train.

There was, you may have noted, a pattern developing. Certain members of the household were trying to misdirect the investigation of the count's murder: Emmie and Sesbania certainly; the countess and Thomas most probably; and the three other servants quite possibly.

Yet what conclusion could be drawn from this was anyone's guess. Were they endeavoring to cover up the facts of the case? Or were they doing it merely for their own amusement? With the three principal females, either seemed equally plausible.

I decided to play along with the charade and keep my own counsel. There's no denying that Emmie's antics are nearly always diverting. What's more, it was the countess who mentioned the casket of correspondence, and I wasn't altogether eager to spoil whatever expectations she may have had. I took the book back to the billiard room, where I found the sergeant sound asleep—presumably keeping the threads untangled.

The code itself was fairly simple to follow. Each new paragraph began with a page number, then there would be anywhere from three to a dozen numbers after that. Still, the work was laborious. I found it easy to lose count, as each of Lacy's snores involved a rhythmically complex series of preparatory snorts.

It was late in the afternoon when I finally had worked out the message and recorded it on the slate. There were some idiosyncrasies in grammar that needed smoothing out, but as near as I could tell, either the French were planning an invasion of Vauxhall, or the Germans one of India. The count was tasked with either learning U.S. postal rates or making contact with the postmaster general's coachman. The message ended with a sensible warning to decline all offers of Charlotte Russe.

On only one point did I feel certain: Emmie'd had a hand in its composition.

Lacy woke sniffing the air just as Geneviève brought us some coffee and pastries.

"Ah! You've cracked it, have you, Mr. Reese? Well, what have you got?"

As he ate, I went through the possibilities. Happily, the sergeant's grasp of world geography rivaled Emmie's own. He found the supposed German invasion of India a wholly reasonable interpretation. I did, however, feel a little bad for the postmaster general's coachman. Revived by the coffee, the sergeant proposed going in search of the man posthaste. He was still looking to finger a servant, however ludicrous the rationale.

"Another German agent! And right in the very bosom of the Republic. He might be the key to the entire mystery."

"Ah, no doubt." I wasn't aware the Republic had a bosom. But if any of its anatomy *were* located in Washington, universal opinion suggested the sergeant was looking at the wrong end. "Perhaps I should stay here. There's still a line or two I haven't worked out. Who knows what other plans are afoot?"

"All right. Get to the bottom of it, Mr. Reese. I'll see you at breakfast."

Among the many curious facts regarding the household, one which still nagged at me was the hiring of

Geneviève through an employment agency known to the countess as purveyors of domestic spies. I decided to go directly to the source. I would put the question to Mr. Chappelle. But rather than risk being overheard on the telephone, I thought it wiser to walk down to his office. It was still located on K Street, according to the city directory—a mere mile away.

I went upstairs to inform Emmie I would be out for the evening. The typing halted as soon as I entered and the leaf of paper disappeared into the drawer.

"Hello, Harry."

She sounded genuinely pleased to see me. It's times like this she's at her most dangerous. I was tempted to check the wardrobe for dagger-wielding highbinders.

"I ran into Dex Peterson on the train down," I told her. "I just remembered that we'd arranged to have dinner tonight."

"Who's he?"

"Fellow from college. Works at the, ah... the Bureau of Weights and Measures. He offered to show me their scales. Care to join us?"

"Sounds fascinating. But I think I'll stay here. Don't be too late...."

"Well, I'll make it as early as possible, but they have quite a few scales."

She got up and gave me a kiss on the cheek. It reminded me of my encounter in the hallway that first night. I turned toward her and put a hand on her hip.

"Maybe I should stay."

"No, go," she said, removing my hand. "And while you're out, you could pick up that perfume." She gave me another kiss. "OK?"

"I'll see what I can do."

She smiled the smile of a coquette—then all but shoved me out the door.

It was bitterly cold outside, but it was a block or two before I noticed. Emmie's spirited good-bye had warmed my cockles. Until that moment I'd had only a vague idea of what one's cockles encompassed—but no longer. Whether it was the story, or the remnants of scent, that French novel had worked its effect on her.

Chappelle was meeting with a client so I took a seat in the empty reception room. The young woman who greeted me took my name, but then went back to her typing and assiduously ignored me. It gave me a feeling of home.

Ten minutes later, Chappelle escorted a prim elderly woman out of his office.

"You may leave it to me, Mrs. Gleason. I have several candidates already in mind and can send the first over in the morning. If she doesn't suit you, I'm sure we have another who will."

"All right. Have her there promptly at half past nine."

"I will make a point of it. Good-bye now."

Chappelle had adjusted to the part of putative businessman remarkably well. When I'd last seen him, he was managing a far more prosaic criminal enterprise.

He greeted me graciously and led me into his office. But it took some doing before he remembered our meeting previously. I asked about his brother, who'd married and moved to France.

"Oh, he's a contented innkeeper. And given his marriage, a likely permanent exile." The brother had married a white woman. "What is it I can do for you today, Mr. Reese?"

"Well, this is a little awkward. But your brother more or less confided the secondary aspect of your business during my last visit."

"Did he?"

"Only after my suspicions were aroused. At present, I'm staying with the Countess von Schnurrenberger."

"Oh, don't forget the *und Kesselheim*." He smiled. "How is Her Ladyship?"

"Well. Though it's hard to imagine her allowing any other condition. But cutting to the chase, I've become acquainted with her maid, Geneviève."

"Ah, Geneviève. Quite a girl. Speaks five languages fluently."

"Well educated for a maid, isn't she?"

"Yes, but she has the sense to keep that to herself."

"What I find curious is that the countess, knowing as she does the dual nature of your business, would allow a young woman of her capabilities into the house."

"Geneviève's position with the countess is a special case. She only snoops *for* the countess, never *on* her. I made very clear to her the sort of woman she would be working for. And so far, she seems to be doing very nicely—save that little matter with the late count."

"What little matter? Had he seduced her?"

"No, quite the opposite. You see, a few months back, the young count came to Washington in order to meet his auntie. He and the countess got along *very* well, for some weeks, I understand. Then some French officer came along and the countess quickly tired of the count. She tried to induce her maid to take up with him, to divert his attention. But the foolish girl had scruples. I found her a place with a widowed congressman and sent Geneviève along at the countess's instruction."

"But she has scruples as well?"

"Good lord, no. Geneviève?" He laughed. "No, apparently the count simply couldn't abide a servant more cosmopolitan than himself. Of course, shortly after, that matter righted itself."

"You mean with his murder?"

"No, no. Before that. Someone else was brought in to divert the count. A writer from New York. The countess led her to believe she'd share her life story with her."

"And *she* succeeded with the count?"

"That was my surmise.... As to the details..." He shrugged. "By the way, how exactly did the count meet his end? The newspapers say only that he was electrocuted."

"He was, but it seems someone had arranged for it."

"Interesting. But given the locus of the crime, I can only pity the poor soul saddled with solving the case." He looked at his watch. "Now, I'm afraid I'm late for a dinner engagement. Perhaps you'd like to come. A benefit for the negro soldiers down in Brownsville."

"The rioters?"

"Rioters! The white officers even swear for them. There was no riot, only the murder of some white men, most likely by some other white men. Now, our dear President Roosevelt, that paragon of rectitude, is throwing a few dozen black men to the lions, for the entertainment of the white southern voter. These are sad days for the dark race, Mr. Reese."

"You said much the same thing last time I was here."

"And things have only gotten worse. It won't be long before the government offices here are segregated."

"You really think things could go that far backward?"

"Wake up! It's happening before your eyes, Mr. Reese." He stopped, then grinned. "I apologize for the oratory. Was there anything else I can help you with?"

"No, that was enough. Thank you."

We rose and he shook my hand. "I'm glad I was able to put your mind at rest."

I saw no point in telling him he'd done just the opposite. The scenario he outlined re Emmie's invitation was a good deal more in keeping with the countess's methods than the alternative explanation she had given Emmie.

I'd been planning to invite Chappelle out for dinner, as my appointment in Georgetown wasn't until ten o'clock. But a benefit for wrongfully condemned men promised to be brimming with meaningful rhetoric and sorely lacking in humorous anecdote. Besides, I could probably best serve the cause by recommending Sesbania take it up.

I walked into Georgetown and found a convivial oyster bar on M Street where I dined on steamed shellfish and warm beer. It was the sort of place Sergeant Lacy would have found useful in acquiring data for his monograph. The conversation was friendly, for the most part, and the crowd only moderately animated. Nonetheless, as the time neared for my appointment with Mrs. Quinlan, certain elements among them became rambunctious. I made my exit simultaneously with a large fellow whose left eye had swollen shut, probably a result of the previous evening's fun. He'd been tossed out by an even larger fellow and subsequently landed headfirst in the amalgamation of half-frozen slush, mud, and manure which lined the curb. Thinking I'd had a hand in his predicament, he eyed me like an affronted Cyclops.

I arrived at the Quinlan house five minutes early and utterly out of breath. I never would have expected such a large fellow could move so quickly.

The lady of the house answered the door herself. She stepped out on the porch and scanned the block before pulling me inside.

"My husband is insanely jealous," she said rather nonchalantly while closing the door. "Here, let me take your things."

I couldn't help but notice—as she reached around my neck and deftly removed my scarf, her cheek, faintly blushing, nearly touching mine—that the scent she was wearing wasn't the inciting one. It was pleasant enough, one might even call it motivating. But it lacked the essential element of provocation. The dressing gown was another matter.

"I've given the servants the night off. We can go up to my sitting room. I've set out some brandy."

I followed her upstairs. She'd pulled up the skirt of her gown and that tightened it about her hips. This was a woman who knew something about walking up stairs.

She had me remove my jacket and sit down on her pillowed couch. Then she poured us a couple large beakers of brandy and knelt on the cushion beside me. I tried keeping the insanely jealous husband firmly in mind, but she wasn't making it easy.

"I'm so glad you came. That evening... it still haunts me."

"I am sorry about the... ah... But the hall was pitch dark."

"Don't be silly. I mean the death of the count."

"Oh, yes, of course. Very sad." I took a gulp of brandy. "I hate to be..."

"Oh, there's no need for secrets between us. I can see you are someone to be trusted. Yes, I was there... to visit the count. My husband was in New York that night. I left here late, so the servants wouldn't know. It was madness.... But I was wild with passion."

"I suppose he *was* handsome."

"Yes, and charming. But it was mainly that scent...."

"The one you were wearing that night?"

"Yes! *Deux nuits d'excès!* It's like a drug.... And just as it promises, a woman may look forward to two nights of unbridled passion, of unimaginable ecstasy!"

"No wonder it's hard to get ahold of."

"Have you been looking for it?"

"My wife smelled it on that book, the one you gave the count."

"I don't remember giving him a book...."

Interestingly, Mrs. Quinlan found it easier to admit adultery than purveying pornography. Maybe she worried she'd be asked to pony up the eight dollars.

"Well, let's just say the count had some arresting reading material. I picked it up and now my wife's under the impression I bought her the book as a Christmas present. Then when she smelled the perfume on it, she became set on that as well. But it can't be had."

"Hmm." She hopped up and went into her bedroom. A minute later she returned. "You may have what's left to give to her." She'd tied a little bow around the vial and dropped it into the pocket of my jacket.

"That's very generous. If what you say..."

"Oh, it's *exactly* as I say. A woman may be sure of two nights of unrestrained lovemaking. But *only* two nights! After that, it is just another perfume. It only provokes the memory of what was!"

"Wow. So you missed your night with the count.... But the second night?"

"The second night, my husband came home. I thought he would do, but then he fell asleep just after dinner.... Poor Lisette."

"Lisette?"

"My maid. I think I frightened... What's that? Oh, no! My husband must be home early! Go! Down the back stairs...."

"Ah, my things..."

"I'll get them to you later.... Go, quickly! And remember: just two nights!"

8

I left Mrs. Quinlan's company feeling plenty warm. The admixture of her finely-aged brandy and her finely-managed form had set my cockles to a rumbling boil. But after a few blocks without hat and coat, the cockles went into hibernation. It was a cold night.

There were several carriages waiting outside the countess's, which meant she was entertaining. In no mood for conversation—and more crucially, lacking an invitation—I went around to the rear entrance. I entered and gently closed the door. From there, I could see Geneviève and Kirsch again washing dishes, while Gustave sat at the table writing out a list of some sort. They seemed not to have heard me come in. Kirsch whispered something to the girl. Then I noticed his hand playfully sneaking a feel of the callipygian maid's finest feature, and her playfully swatting it away. Gustave noticed too. He looked discomfited, but maybe the rich young widow on Kalorama was causing him trouble. Given her three known attributes, I suppose she could afford to.

I crept up the back stairs. From the servants' hall, I could hear someone in the count's bedroom. I peered in through the keyhole. There was only a dim light, but it was enough. Two of the more spirited guests had paired off and were in active conference. After a few minutes, I crept through to the main hall and there saw Sesbania glued to the keyhole of the other door.

"Aren't you a little young for peep shows?"

"Oh!" It was the one and only time *I* surprised *her*. "I thought perhaps that gambler had returned."

"The one who conveniently left his dice as a calling card?"

"They must have fallen out of his pocket as he climbed in the window. It was your idea...."

"What was my idea?"

"That the gambler who had lost money to Captain Dumont might have come to retrieve it and knocked out Sergeant Lacy."

"So you were eavesdropping? Then you went and got the dice.... Who helped you with the ladder?"

"No one helped me!" she shouted. I'd insulted her. Not by suggesting she was guilty, only that she'd have required help. By now, you ought to understand why her parents preferred traveling without her.

Her indignant cry had not gone unnoticed. An exclamation from inside the count's room followed immediately. Sesbania vanished and a second later a half-naked woman clutching shoes and gown opened the door. She seemed surprised to see me. She gave me an awkward smile and sprinted for the bathroom. My curiosity piqued, I turned back to see a surprisingly well-groomed man at the door. He was straightening his tie, and seemed not nearly so disconcerted at seeing me as I was him. It was Dex Peterson, the fellow I'd told Emmie I was meeting for dinner.

"Hello, Harry. I met your wife earlier. Nice girl."

"Thanks, Dex. How about you? Married?"

"No. No time for women. Politics is a full-time business. Why are you hiding up here?"

"Just came in, not really in the mood for socializing."

"Sure, I know what you mean: pure drudgery. Listen, I better head back down, before... ah.... Say, give me a call while you're in town."

"Sure thing."

I'd also misled Emmie about Dex's employment. I'd deliberately made the evening sound as dull as possible, in case she'd have wanted to come along. The only weights and measures Dex Peterson concerned himself with belonged to whatever females were currently on offer. He was a lawyer, one of countless Washington lobbyists who work hard at debauching the body politic. In a pinch, of course, *any* body would do.

I stepped across to our room and placed the vial of perfume on Emmie's night stand—right beside *Gamiani*. Once in bed, I turned out the light, figuring I'd surprise her on her return.

After about half an hour, I became bored with the game. I turned the light back on and found my place in *The Sign of Four*. But it just couldn't hold my interest. After the lively goings-on of the evening, Watson's storytelling came off as rather listless. Even his courtship of Miss Morstan lacked vitality. Couldn't he have at least tried something during that long cab ride back to town? It was just the two of them, at night, and god knows she was in want of comforting.

I set down Conan Doyle's book and thought I'd take a stab at *Gamiani*. It had certainly held Emmie's attention. She'd even underlined certain passages in pencil. I could only make out about every other word or so, but then I noticed Emmie must have had some trouble herself. She'd borrowed a French-English dictionary. It was still slow going, but luckily the author didn't waste much time on the preliminaries.

The story opens with the Countess Gamiani hosting a ball. At its conclusion, she offers a stranded young woman lodging for the night. Next, she inveigles the girl into sharing her bed. And this is a countess who knows how to inveigle. She puts body and soul into it. Meanwhile, the narrator hides himself in the countess's dressing room, from which he can observe the bedroom. He is not disappointed.

The hostess continues her inveigling, for want of a better word, until she and the girl are both equally energized. Then the countess breaks into a salacious dance, thus leaving the energized girl unattended. The narrator seizes his opening, and soon comes upon hers as well. Now that he's entered into the revels, it isn't long before things come to a head—several times, in fact.

Not much of a plot, perhaps, but riveting nonetheless. I was still engaged in translating when Emmie surprised me.

"Harry! When did you get here?"

"A while ago. Came up the back."

She eyed me with mild suspicion. "Where were you tonight?"

"Well, it turns out old Dex stood me up. I had to get my tour of the weights and measures from the janitor. Nice old guy. We played a few games of dominoes, and before I knew it, it was after eleven."

She made one of her noises. "Dominoes..."

"Has the party broken up?"

"Yes, finally. It's nearly five."

She got into her nightgown and was about to crawl into bed when she caught sight of the perfume bottle.

"Oh. You got it...." She untied the ribbon and held the stopper to her nose. A look came over her. She dabbed some behind her ears. Then her wrists. She shivered. Her nightgown dropped to the floor. Now she was running the stopper down her certain bit of anatomy....

Suddenly, a blood-curdling cry emanated from somewhere below. Emmie seemed completely oblivious and I followed her lead. She let loose her hair, then swung her head from side to side....

"Oh, Harry..." There was an unfamiliar quality to her voice. Quite arresting.

Then someone was pounding on the door. "Mr. Reese! Please, Mr. Reese! It's so horrible...."

"It's Geneviève," I said.

"Geneviève...," Emmie echoed mechanically. She slipped under the covers....

"Harry! Get up this instant." This time, it was the countess.

By then Emmie had her hands on my thighs. Her hair was tousled and there was a hint of the demonic in her eyes... as if some alien being, some succubus, had taken her form. Were it up to me, she could have the keys.

"*Now*, Harry!" The countess was still at the door. "Or I'll open it myself."

Reluctantly, I unpinned myself from the mad nymph and threw on my robe. Though I'm not sure the word reluctantly adequately describes my feelings at that moment. I opened the door and Geneviève fell upon me. She was hysterical, blabbering in French and English something about murder.

"*Tais-toi!*" The countess spun her around and slapped her, then pushed her into our room. "Emmie, look after the girl." She closed the door and turned to me.

"It seems Gustave has killed that damn valet. I knew he was trouble the minute I saw him."

"Gustave?"

"Gustave! Don't be an ass. You'll need to help Thomas dispose of the body."

"Dispose of the body?"

"Have you gone deaf?"

"Wouldn't summoning the police be a more prudent course?"

She looked at me as if I'd just proposed we go for a naked swim in the icy Potomac. "Harry, if I lose my cook because of your slothfulness, you will regret it for the rest of your short life. Is that understood?"

"Ah... where's the body?"

"In the kitchen. Thomas is getting out the auto."

"I'll come, too." It was Sesbania.

"No you won't," her mentor told her. "This is work best left to men."

"Maybe men with some experience..."

"It's simple, Harry. Thomas knows what to do."

I didn't doubt that. I turned to the girl. "I'm afraid I misplaced my hat and coat earlier this evening. I don't suppose you could spare something from your collection?"

"I'm afraid... No, wait. I've just the things. Downstairs."

We all three went down to the kitchen, and all three froze at the door.

"There he is," the countess said rather unnecessarily.

This time, Gustave had chosen a more traditional weapon than a chicken bone in a soft dessert. There was a meat cleaver embedded in the German's chest.

Contrary to the countess's earlier assertion, I have no affinity for corpses—particularly not ones with meat cleavers attached. I reflexively turned away from the gruesome scene. The two females were not so squeamish.

"I would have thought there'd be more blood splattered about," Sesbania said.

"Oh, it all comes down to where you plant the blade," the countess told her. From her tone, she might have been sharing a tip on the proper brewing of coffee.

"Where's Gustave?" I asked.

"I sent him to his room."

"He won't be coming along?"

"No, he's far too upset to be of any use."

"Poor fellow."

Thomas came in the back door bearing an oilcloth. He removed the cleaver and rinsed it in the sink. I expected it would be back to more mundane duties on the morrow.

After we'd wrapped up the body, Sesbania went over and retrieved a very handsome cashmere coat and a fur hat from the rack by the back door, then presented them to me.

"Whose are these?"

"Herr Kirsch's."

"Well, I don't suppose he'll be missing them."

"Oh, but I will want them back later."

This kid never let up. "Where are we taking the corpse?" I asked the countess.

"Leave that to Thomas. Good luck."

She led Sesbania upstairs.

Thankfully, Kirsch was of a fortunate physique. Not only was he fairly easy to carry, but his coat fit like a glove. We stowed him in the back of the auto and then

Thomas drove in the general direction of the river. He suggested an underused wharf he knew of on the Georgetown waterfront. Unqualified to offer an opinion of my own, I made no objection.

"There's never anyone about at night," he assured me.

I didn't ask how he came by that knowledge.

We drove to the foot of the wharf and had the body half out of the car when we heard a police whistle. There was a cop trotting up the street, calling to us. We stuffed the body back in and Thomas drove downriver past the policeman. Then he made a sharp left and stopped on a little bridge over the canal. I recognized the location from our last trip. It was here that Emmie had spotted a drunken Irishman she hoped was a corpse. But that's another story.

"Quickly!" he said.

We got the body out and Thomas tied on some lead piping he'd had the forethought to bring along. It made a rather loud sound on hitting the water. We were just preparing to leave when a second auto came upon us from the direction of the wharf. A fellow stuck his head out the window.

"Kirsch! *Was machen Sie?* Kirsch! *Kommen Sie her!*"

Thomas looked at me, then the fur hat.

"I think we should leave."

I was in the car before he'd finished his sentence. He took a turn to the west, then drove north two or three miles. After that, I lost all sense of direction.

"I'd say you definitely lost them."

"Yes," he said. "But they recognized that hat and coat as Kirsch's. They will be waiting at the house."

"Who were they? Seemed to speaking in German."

"I don't know. Maybe his friends."

"Didn't sound terribly friendly."

"No, they didn't. We must be careful, or we could endanger the countess."

"Yes, we mustn't endanger the countess."

Just then the car sputtered to a halt.

"We are out of petrol. We will need to walk from here."

"How far is it?"

"Not far. We can go down through the park."

Not far, of course, is a relative term. Let's just say Thomas and I held contrary opinions on the matter. He led me down a steep path and into a wooded valley, then we took off our shoes and waded across what I assume was Rock Creek. The water wasn't at all deep, but it was plenty bracing. There was another half mile or so of woods to get through, then a steep climb up. Once we'd ascended, I noticed the large bridge just a block away. It was the one used by the street car line that ran to Chevy Chase.

"Wouldn't it have been easier to cross the gorge at the bridge?"

"Yes, but easier to have been seen as well. Those men believe you are Kirsch. We must make sure they don't get close enough to see that you are not. If they approached us on the bridge, there would be no place to hide."

I'd come to find Thomas's devotion to duty rather trying.

He led me via side streets and alleys back to where we could see the house. The sun was up by now and we easily spotted the car we'd encountered in Georgetown parked just down the street. A man was pacing up and down the block.

"How are we going to get by them?" I asked.

"Look! There, on the porch."

Only then did I notice Sergeant Lacy. He was peering in a window.

"Come for his breakfast," I said.

"I will go talk to him. They will not interfere with a policeman. You stay hidden until it is safe. And say nothing to give away your identity. They must be made to think Kirsch is alive."

"Are you sure you don't know who they are?"

"I fear they are agents of the Kaiser."

"What do they have to do with Kirsch?"

He shrugged, then pulled down my hat and turned up my collar to better conceal my face.

I stood there shivering while he trotted across the street and began speaking with Lacy. He pointed at the car. Lacy started down the steps.

The man who'd been pacing went to the car to consult with his fellows. A moment later, they drove off. Just as Thomas had anticipated, they seemed to have recognized the policeman.

I emerged and Lacy walked toward me.

"Mr. Reese? Is that you?"

"Yes. Out for a little air."

"That butler's acting a little queer. Told me the men in that car seemed to be spying on the house."

"I suppose we have to expect things of that sort. What with the coded messages and whatnot."

Lacy didn't hide his disappointment at finding the sideboard empty.

"Sunday morning," I told him. "I suppose everyone

rises a little late." Especially on days following executions.

"No rest for ourselves, though, Mr. Reese."

"No, no rest at all, in fact. I'll go check on the kitchen."

Gustave was there, looking surprisingly well rested. He'd made coffee and had begun filling platters.

"No trouble sleeping last night?" I asked.

He looked back at me blankly.

"Never mind. Where's Geneviève?"

He shrugged. You might think the dispatching of the valet would at least have made him a little less haughty.

"Sergeant Lacy's waiting for his breakfast. You can take it out to him. He doesn't know about last night—yet."

He gave me another bewildered look, so I pantomimed the serving. Then I went up the back stairs and crossed the hall to our room. Both Emmie and Geneviève were asleep on the bed. It was a scene that invited speculation. Beyond that, I'll leave to your imagination. Mine was already working on the sorts of scenarios which could have brought them to such an entanglement.

"Oh! Mr. Reese... I... It was..."

"Ah, never mind. You better get dressed and go down and help with breakfast."

"Yes..." She put on her frock and slipped quietly out of the room.

It'd been a long, exhausting night—but my imagination wasn't even winded. The tête-à-tête with Emmie immediately previous to my departure was etched pretty deeply on my mind. Throughout the frigid morning adventure, I'd been envisioning our reunion and its myriad possibilities (only two of which involved the

French maid). I was hoping to find Emmie with her engine still running. But she was out cold. I gave her a warm kiss. Nothing. It appeared that the ecstasy abated with the rising of the sun. Amazing stuff, this perfume—but it certainly came with a lot of caveats.

I went down the hall for a quick bath. When I returned, Emmie was in the same position. I dressed and joined Lacy. Sesbania was there fabricating a story to explain Kirsch's exit from the house.

"Abducted by foreign agents?" the sergeant asked.

"Yes. I was out for a walk and I saw him dragged away. They put him in the back of their automobile and drove off. They may have been Russians who hope to get those coded messages you found in the count's room."

"Do they, now?"

"Oh, yes. But I think it's more likely they were German agents who suspect Herr Kirsch killed the count. He was almost certainly working for the Kaiser as well—though it is possible he was secretly betraying the Kaiser to the Czar."

A day before, her theory would have struck me as perfectly ludicrous.

"Did you know they are first cousins?" she asked Lacy.

"Who?"

"The Kaiser and the Czar. Both grandsons of Queen Victoria. Anyway, I don't think we'll be seeing any more of Herr Kirsch.... Not unless they failed to weight the body properly."

"Weight the body?"

"When they threw it in the river. Otherwise it will pop right back up. Isn't that right, Mr. Reese?"

Lacy turned briefly in my direction, then went back to his sausage.

I gave my arch little tormentor a threatening look. She just smiled and winked.

May God help the poor soul who takes her to the altar.

9

"Well, Mr. Reese. This news about the valet certainly muddies the waters, doesn't it?"

"Any muddier and we could walk across to the other side."

I wouldn't have minded a morning nap, but Lacy had already engaged the one comfortable chair the billiard room had to offer.

"Did you learn anything else after I left yesterday?"

"Anything else?"

"You said you had some more code to decipher." He picked up the book and pulled the page of numbers out. A second piece of paper fluttered to the floor.

I picked it up. It was like the first, a page filled with numbers divided into paragraphs—only, it hadn't been in the book when I last left the room.

"This is it. I was distracted last evening. I'll get to work on it now."

While I decoded, Lacy went to work untangling threads. Mercifully, his snoring came not so syncopated as the day before.

"Mr. Reese?" Geneviève had poked her head in the door. "Can I have a word?" she whispered.

I joined her and quietly closed the door.

"I only want to explain.... About what happened last night...."

"With my wife? Well, one hates to appear nosy, but since you mention it...." Certain scenes in *Gamiani* had, among other things, aroused my curiosity. And I felt sure

Emmie wouldn't be providing any clarification. Any details the maid wanted to share by way of a confession would be welcome—absolution assured.

"With your wife? She... she only comforted me. If you remember, I was very upset.... No, I mean what happened with Gustave and Herr Kirsch."

"I think I have a good idea what that was about. You lied about Gustave, didn't you? He really *was* jealous."

"Jealous? Oh, no. *I* wasn't the cause. Or, rather, not in that way. But I suppose I did bring it about."

"How?"

"Well, we were the four of us—Gustave, Thomas, and Herr Kirsch and I—cleaning up after the last of the guests went off. While we'd been waiting, we'd had some wine. Quite a lot of wine. And I should mention, Gustave has a tendency to get... emotional when he's had a lot of wine. Well, there was a piece of strudel left untouched. I carried it into the kitchen and ate some. Then I said to Herr Kirsch, 'Isn't Gustave's strudel the best in the world?' And he said, 'Pish! For a Frenchman...'"

"For a Frenchman *what?*"

"That was as far as he got...."

"I'm glad I didn't complain about the runny eggs."

"I don't think Gustave meant to kill him."

"No? Perhaps he saw the cleaver as a mere rhetorical device?"

"*Pardon?*"

"Never mind. Tell me, what did you really know about Herr Kirsch?"

"A little stiff, like all Germans. And very secretive. I often saw him listening to conversations. Once I found him near the door of the countess's study. He told me he was looking for the count's walking stick. When I told this to the countess, she directed me to keep an eye on him."

"So that's why you were flirting with him?"

"*Oui*. So I could watch him without suspicion."

"Tell me honestly, who was it who killed the count?"

"I swear, I don't know!"

"But you must have suspicions."

"Not really. The countess had grown tired of him, but there was no hatred. Captain Dumont would tease him sometimes about his formality, but they often spent hours playing billiards, or cards. Gustave didn't like him, but he likes so few men."

"And only kills some of them.... What about Kirsch?"

"He seemed protective of his employer. I never saw him angry at the count."

"Did you ever see him meet with anyone from outside the house?"

"The count or Herr Kirsch?"

"Either."

"The count frequently socialized with others. He sometimes dined at various embassies. When the weather permitted, he would go riding. And then there were the ladies.... He went out sometimes, late at night."

"And Kirsch?"

"Well, a servant has little time to himself. He went out sometimes, when the count was off somewhere. Once, late at night. But we never went out together. I do remember one evening he received a telephone call."

"A friend?"

"No, not a friend. He spoke very respectfully, almost seemed nervous."

"You speak German, don't you? What was it about?"

"He said nothing of significance. Just yes, no, soon...."

"As if he suspected someone was listening."

"Perhaps. I think now I should go. We've a large dinner to prepare."

She went back to the kitchen and I got back to my deciphering. I was beginning to enjoy the game. And in another hour, I had the solution. This message informed the count of a new assignment: he was to determine the route of the Japanese army's invasion of the South American mainland. It seems the fellow on the Chrysanthemum Throne had set his heart on the legendary El Dorado.

The count was further advised that Dumont was a French spy and seeking the same information. The sender suggested he should exploit the captain's weakness for gambling in order to compromise him. A pair of loaded dice would be arriving under separate cover. Next, the order to make contact with the postmaster general's coachman was rescinded. He was in reality an agent of the American government trying to expose the Germans' efforts. The last line offered a sensible warning: beware of frayed lamp cords.

It sounded as if Emmie had wanted to tie up all the loose ends—then inadvertently created a few more.

When Lacy awoke for the late-morning coffee, I shared what I had learned.

"An American agent... I suppose that explains why the postmaster general was so irate," he said. "Told me to keep my idiotic suspicions to myself. I assumed it was a bluff, and it seems I was right. We've entered deep waters now, Mr. Reese."

"Deep and muddy."

"Indeed. From now on, we'll be threading a needle."

"So you plan to proceed with the investigation?"

"Why not?"

"Well, all this foreign intrigue. Dangerous ground for a civil servant, isn't it?"

"Yes, caution is in order. But suppose I can uncover the ring of spies? Think what a feather in my cap that would be."

"Especially if you do it before the postmaster general's coachman."

"Yes, that would put him in his place. Now, if we can solve the abduction of Kirsch, I believe the rest will fall into place."

"Will it?"

"Of course. And once we deduce *who* abducted him, the *why* will be obvious. What we need to do now is lay out all the possibilities."

"All of them?"

"Within reason, of course. First, given what we know about the count and Dumont, we can reasonably presume that whoever abducted Kirsch was likewise working for a foreign government."

"What about the postmaster general's coachman?"

"No, if it were him behind it, there would have been no witnesses."

"Ah. A master of the subtle. How do we determine which foreign government?"

"There can't be more than thirty or forty foreign missions in town. And we can leave out the Abyssinians, as the girl would have mentioned their color if they'd abducted Kirsch. And the Chinese, Japanese, Siamese..."

"Ottomans?"

"Oh, they're a sly bunch—can't count them out. Or the Mexicans. Met a blonde one just last year. You would've sworn she was white."

"Can't get any slyer than that."

We spent the next few hours on our conundrum without making much progress. We got bogged down in trying to decide the racial makeup of the South American republics. The crux rested on whether they were Europeans who interbred with mulatto Indians, or mulattoes who interbred with Indians. Threading needles while treading deep and muddy waters is a lot more difficult than you might expect.

Sunday dinner was served at four and the table was a large one. Dr. Gillette and his wife were first to arrive. I assumed the countess flattered him with an invitation in order to maintain his allegiance. Or perhaps Mrs. Gillette's caustic tongue amused her. I remembered during our last visit hearing her describe her recently deceased father as a greedy war profiteer—harsh words for an only child and sole heir. But don't think she was made of stone. She did manage to forgive his fortune.

Also attending were a particular senator and his not so particular young wife—a proclivity she shared (and who knows what else) with the late count. Mrs. Quinlan smiled warmly when we were introduced, but otherwise gave no hint of our previous encounters. Her husband also struck me as familiar, but only because he exemplified a type: that singular mix of mental insularity and egotistic self-importance which so often marks men of high standing.

The table talk consisted mainly of complaints about the crowded stores and changeable weather. Even before the soup was cleared, the countess had become visibly tired of the conversation. She now endeavored to enliven it.

"I don't think I gave Sergeant Lacy the introduction

he deserves. You see, he is well known as a rival of Mr. Sherlock Holmes."

"Not rival, Your Ladyship," he corrected. "Merely a fellow practitioner. Many of his methods are similar to mine."

"And your habits?" Mrs. Gillette asked.

"Habits? Which habits in particular?"

"Do you likewise have a fondness for cocaine?"

"That would be frowned on. And I'm not sure it would agree with me."

"Mr. Holmes seems to find it very agreeable."

"Well, I don't have the luxury of lounging about all day in my dressing gown. There are, I think you'll admit, certain of Mr. Holmes's traits which serve no good."

"How can you be sure until you try it?" Sesbania asked.

"My powers of deduction."

The girl smirked. "He also doesn't play the violin," she noted, with only the barest hint of reproof.

"An irritating habit," the countess said. "My late husband played the violin. And quite badly. He'd been planning to give us a recital the evening he passed away...."

"I'm sure just a coincidence," Mrs. Gillette half-whispered.

"I couldn't agree more, Your Ladyship. By the way, I've brought the monograph I told you of, if you would care to take a look."

"How lovely. But let's save that for coffee."

"What can you tell us about your investigation into the murder of the count?" Mrs. Gillette asked him. "I mean, the most recent count ...of course." She almost smiled, but then thought better of it.

The doctor took out his handkerchief and patted his

glistening brow. It had good cause to glisten. If his wife was going to send playful barbs the way of the countess, they'd both better be vigilant when eating their dessert.

"I believe we are on the cusp of a solution," Lacy announced.

"Then you expect to make an arrest?" The sergeant's assertion seemed to have caught Emmie off guard.

"If it's within my power.... But as I'm sure all of you are aware, sometimes our hands are tied by the niceties required of a city hosting foreign missions. I can give you a for instance. Just last year, the ambassador of... Well, the ambassador of a Latin republic caught his wife with the chauffeur, *in flagrante delicto*. Colored."

"Colored?" Mrs. Quinlan asked.

"The chauffeur. Hard to tell, some of them, but he was as African as I am American. Well, the ambassador fetched a revolver and shot them both."

"And he escaped punishment?"

"Not entirely. He was able to leave Washington on his diplomatic passport. But as fate would have it, there'd been a coup in his absence and the new masters felt unsure of his loyalty. Didn't make it off the boat."

"The Lord works in mysterious ways," Mrs. Gillette mused.

"Don't I know it, Mrs. G."

"Tell me, do you also share Mr. Holmes's powers of inference?" Mrs. Quinlan queried.

"Powers of inference?"

"Well, the way Mr. Holmes can describe a person's life in such detail after a simple examination of a hat, or a walking stick. Or an encounter lasting mere minutes. As an example, having just met me, what can you tell the others about *my* past?"

"I would say you are a lady of aristocratic blood. Perhaps you are unaware, but somewhere in your past was a royal personage."

Not bad, I thought. A conjecture of royal blood was nothing but riskless flattery.

The old senator chuckled. "That's just Boston snobbery you've hit on."

"No, John. I'm afraid what the sergeant says is true."

"What? You never mentioned it before."

"I didn't tell you because I was afraid to!" Mrs. Quinlan, I suspect, had studied dramatics.

"No need to be afraid. Why, when garnering votes, it wouldn't hurt…"

"No, John. I'm afraid it isn't some prestigious house of Europe. My grandfather was a king, to be sure…. But a king of a different sort."

"What are you talking about?"

"Well, I suppose there's no use trying to hide it now. My mother's father was a king of the gypsies!"

"The gypsies?"

"Yes, it's a secret I've kept hidden since my childhood."

"I suppose that does explain your mother's complexion. A bit awkward…. But it needn't go further…. I'm sure we can trust our friends here to maintain discretion."

"Oh, I'm afraid that's the one course never partaken of at a Washington table," Mrs. Gillette told him.

The old man blushed. His comely wife reached across the table and patted his hand. "Perhaps it's better we forget about votes, and Washington. Remember, that ambassadorship is still open…."

"Yes, you may be right."

The successful politician is a malleable lump of clay;

he wears the fingerprints of his keepers as a mantle. Mrs. Quinlan's were all over the old man.

The countess lifted her glass and toasted the acumen of the sergeant. Lacy basked contentedly in the attention, but no further mention was made of his monograph on spittle.

It was almost six when the guests left the table. The doctor, clearly relieved to have survived the meal, hurried his wife outside. Meanwhile, Mrs. Quinlan asked me to help her with her coat. As I did, she whispered in my ear, "I had the coachman take your things to the kitchen. How was last night?"

"From all indications eventful, but I unfortunately missed it. I'd been sent out of the house on a mission."

"Then my advice is not to let your wife out of your sight until sunup tomorrow."

Once the guests had departed, Lacy insisted I return to the billiard room with him. "My wife's train gets in at eight, so we have an hour to tie things up."

"I thought we were still threading needles in deep, muddy waters?"

"It all came clear to me, over the cognac."

Somehow I wasn't surprised. With his wife's return, the sergeant would be eating at home.

"Then who was it who killed the count?" I asked.

"Dumont. They were both spies after the same bit of goods."

"You mean, the lubricious lips?"

"The plans of the Japanese invasion. Dumont wanted an open field. He knew the maid would be bringing the count his breakfast, so he set his trap the night before."

"And who set it off?"

"No doubt a female visitor, unaware of the Frenchman's machine. But who, we will never know." The look he gave me, however, contradicted his words; he still suspected the lubricious lips. "But what does it matter who?"

"Maybe the countess…"

"Hardly the more likely lady," he smiled.

"But as you so aptly pointed out, what does it matter? Well, this is tying up nicely…. Who was it then who knocked you out?"

"That we do know: the gambler."

"Ah, of course. And Kirsch? Who abducted him?"

"I now believe it was men in the employ of the coachman, after all."

"The postmaster general's coachman?"

"He's at the center of it. *And* he's untouchable…. Oh, you will have quite a time writing this up, Mr. Reese."

"Perhaps if I leave out the inconvenient details and concentrate on your inimitable technique?"

"Excellent idea. In fact, I'll lend you the monograph. Maybe you can work my encyclopedic knowledge of expectoration into the case?"

"I don't see why not."

Thomas poked his head in the door. "The countess wishes a moment of your time, Mr. Reese."

We went up to her study. The butler shut the door, then stood off to one side.

"Thomas tells me we've had a bit of luck."

"Yes, Sergeant Lacy seems to be throwing in the towel. He won't be bothering you anymore."

"Rather sudden, isn't it?"

"Well, I suspect his diligence the last few days was influenced by the fact his wife was out of town. He was more interested in your larder than your murder."

"Good. But that wasn't the bit of luck I was speaking of. Thomas says those Germans seemed to think you were Kirsch."

"Yes, but they went off this morning."

"Look." She gestured toward the window.

Parked out front was the same car we had encountered the night before.

"As long as they think Kirsch is holed up here, they'll be at my doorstep. You need to lure them away."

"Lure them away?"

"Thomas will bring around the auto and pick you up in front of the house. That way they'll be sure to see you in Kirsch's hat and coat. He will then drive you to the railway station. There you will board the eight o'clock train going south. Once it is underway, you may discreetly discard the coat and hat. When you reach Alexandria, leave the train at the last possible moment. Thomas will pick you up there in the auto. Is that all clear?"

"It's clear enough, just sounds a little risky."

"Do as you are told, and all will be well. But under no circumstances allow yourself to be followed back. Good luck, Harry."

I went down the hall to our room. It was my first moment with Emmie alone and awake since the previous night. She was already in her nightgown.

"Let's go to bed early, Harry. I'm exhausted." Her eyes were looking languid, but I could see a hint of the demon within.

"I'm not surprised."

"What do you mean?"

"When I came in this morning, you and Geneviève..."

"Geneviève? I'm... I'm sure nothing happened."

Somehow, she didn't sound all that convinced. But after one whiff of the inciting perfume, I was willing to forgive and forget—well, perhaps not forget.

By now she had me entwined. Reluctantly, I loosened her grip. (Reluctant departures, you may have noticed, were something of a recurring motif during my sojourn in Washington.)

"I have to go out. On a commission for the countess."

"Again? Who's been killed now?"

"No one, so far as I know. Just a little deception. I'll be back before midnight."

"Midnight? That's hours from now."

"Think how I feel. I spent last night with Thomas."

"Thomas?"

Now *she* had something to think about.

10

A vague premonition came upon me. It concerned the evening's adventure and it quite efficiently put the kibosh on what little enthusiasm I'd managed to muster for the business. To be fair, it only started out as vague. It ended all too distinctly—with me being tossed from a moving train into the icy Potomac.

Things began well enough. Since the train I was to catch was the same one his wife was arriving on, I offered the sergeant a ride to the station. Thomas brought the car around, then Lacy and I—in my guise as Herr Kirsch—hurried aboard. The German agents were still waiting in the street. Just as I hoped, they were once again held in check by the presence of the lawman—but only for the moment. When I looked back, I saw their car pull away from the curb.

"Kind of sudden, your leaving town, isn't it, Mr. Reese?" the sergeant asked.

"Well, with the case all wrapped up, I thought I'd spend some time with my aunt."

"Oh, where's she?"

"Where? Eh, down ole Virginny way."

"Charlottesville," Thomas helpfully added.

"That's right," I said. "She runs an all-night cribbage parlor—very popular with the college boys."

"Any money in that?"

"The way she plays the game there is...."

"You seem to be doing well yourself. I'll bet that coat set you back a few dollars. And the hat. Beaver?"

"Sable, I believe. Coat's cashmere. It is nice, isn't it? ...But ...ah, to tell the truth, I'm due for a change."

"Look almost new."

"Only second time I've worn them out.... But really, they attract too much attention for a fellow in my line. I think I'll go next for something less ostentatious. Like yours, say. Handsome, but unassuming. And plenty comfortable, I imagine."

"Comfortable, but dull."

"Well, I suppose... If you're amenable... We could maybe swap. My cashmere and sable for your tweed and derby?"

"No, I don't think yours would fit me." He patted his stomach. "The missus feeds me too well."

"Nonsense. I had to have it taken in. You just have it taken back out."

I took off the hat and he tried it on.

"Never felt a hat like that."

"And fits perfectly." I started on the coat. Thomas looked back at me and shook his head. Of course, he wasn't the one who was going to be thrown from a moving train into the icy Potomac.

"Wouldn't I like to, Mr. Reese. But what would happen if I show up at the station without the hat and coat the wife bought me for Christmas? She wouldn't talk to me 'til spring."

"Some might say that would be reason enough."

We'd come to a stop. Thomas opened the door and Lacy tumbled out. When I followed bareheaded, Thomas jabbed the barrel of a revolver into my ribs.

"The hat. You will follow instructions exactly. *Klar?*"

"*Ja, klar.* But go easy with the gun. This is cashmere, you know."

"Here is your ticket. Stay close to the policeman and board the train at the last moment. I will meet you in Alexandria in not less than twenty minutes, nor more than thirty. But make absolutely certain you are not followed off the train."

We caught up with Lacy and then saw two of the German agents emerge from the darkness. The train was just arriving when we reached the platform. I stood as close to Lacy as possible, with Thomas on my other side reminding me of his pistol via periodic jabs to the ribs. When Mrs. Lacy emerged, we approached her as a unit. It felt rather comical—except for the gun barrel poking my ribs.

His lady was the demonstrative type and I sensed Lacy wished for me to leave them alone after he twice in quick succession brought his left heel down sharply on the toes of my right foot. But I stuck with them until the train had almost passed us.

"Go!" Thomas shouted—then gave me one last poke in case I'd forgotten about the pistol.

I made the tail end of the last car. One of the Germans witnessed my leap from the platform, but his associate had vanished. The moment I entered the overheated coach, I doffed the hat and coat and set them on an empty seat. No one seemed to take notice, so I walked forward to the next car and took the window seat next to a fellow who had the look of jovial idiocy which marks the salesman. Drummers think themselves the raconteurs of the American road, and for the moment, I craved the cover of conversation. Only when he'd unwound the first of what promised to be a long string of hackneyed anecdotes did I dare breathe.

I continued in this easy state all through his belabored yarn about a one-armed barber in Roanoke, and right up to the moment when I spotted the German agent I hadn't accounted for back on the platform. He was walking down the aisle toward me, scanning the passengers on either side. Then he stopped dead in his tracks—not looking at me, but at someone at the rear of the car. I glanced over my shoulder. There was a fellow coming up the aisle wearing the cashmere and sable.

The German hurried toward him, then pushed him out into the vestibule between the cars. The train was then over the river, and though I heard no splash, I thought it very likely the fellow regretted his pilferage.

Now out of danger, I abandoned the droning bore and moved to the front of the train. When the conductor called out, "Alexandria. Next stop, Alexandria," I went out to the vestibule and climbed down to the last step. It was another cold night, but my warm relief at having made it over the icy river mitigated its effects.

As soon as the train slowed enough to make it safe, I hopped off, then walked quickly down the platform. I heard steps behind me, someone running. I picked up my pace. Then a man to my rear yelled, "*Ihm!*" A fellow emerged from the shadows on my right and I again felt a barrel in my ribs. His comrade came up from behind and grabbed my arm.

"No tricks," he whispered in my ear. He'd had onions with dinner.

He had the hat and coat he'd retrieved from the thief and insisted I put them on. The two of them escorted me out of the station and into a waiting sedan. Just as we were getting in, Thomas drove up. Our eyes met. Then—evidently not displeased with the adventure's outcome—he drove off. I was coming to dislike Thomas.

I turned to the fellow sitting beside me in the backseat. "Look, you're making a big mistake. You could save yourself a good deal of embarrassment..."

"Quiet!" He jabbed the gun a little deeper into my ribs. Frankly, I was coming to dislike Germans generally.

We traveled along the river, then crossed a long bridge and reentered Washington. We passed the Treasury building, then continued a long way northward until we were in a part of the city I wasn't familiar with. The houses sat further apart and there were woods off to the left. They pulled up a drive. It led to a large house, set back from the road.

"Out!"

They brought me down into a decidedly nasty basement. I'll admit I'd been in ranker, more repugnant basements, but the unpleasant circumstances made it impossible for me to maintain objectivity on the matter. They pushed me into a chair and tied me down with typical German thoroughness. The chair itself, I noticed, was bolted to the floor. I took that as a bad sign. It's my experience that people generally don't bolt furniture to floors without some reason, and I couldn't imagine one that didn't end badly for yours truly.

They turned on a bright light and shined it directly into my face. I could see nothing, but heard someone come down wooden stairs. This new fellow interrogated my abductors in German. The gist of it seemed to be that he had expected Herr Kirsch and wasn't altogether pleased with the substitution. Then he spoke to me in English.

"Where is Kirsch?"

"Honestly, I have no idea what you're talking about."

"Do you think we are fools? You are wearing his hat and coat."

"Your henchman forced me to."

One of the underlings explained something in German.

"You left the house wearing them, then removed them on the train. The man who stole them identified you."

"He must have mistaken me for someone else."

"Then where is your own overcoat?"

That wasn't a question I'd anticipated. I tried to come up with a reasonable answer, but he wasn't the patient sort of interrogator.

"Tell us what happened to Kirsch!"

One of the other fellows began working some device in the background. It made a hideous noise, like metal scraping metal. I feared they'd been caught short of lubricants and might be sizing me up as an alternative.

"All right," I said. "But you aren't going to like it."

"Quit stalling and talk!"

"Well, it seems Herr Kirsch took it upon himself to offer the cook a critique of his strudel."

"What cook?"

"The cook there at the countess's house. He's a Frenchman, and rather sensitive. And apparently the wine had been flowing. Gustave—the cook—tends to get extra sensitive when he's had a lot."

"Tell me about Kirsch!"

"Well, as luck would have it, there was a meat cleaver in easy reach. Just as Herr Kirsch began expressing his opinion of the strudel, Gustave cut him short."

"Never have I heard such a ridiculous story."

"That right? Then I assume you missed the half-dozen previous installments."

"Quit babbling! If Kirsch was killed, why has there been nothing reported in the newspaper?"

"The countess prefers to avoid notoriety of that sort."

"Then what happened to the corpse?"

"You aren't going to like this either. We disposed of it. You'll find it in the canal, right where your fellows encountered us last night."

They held another conversation in German. It ended with an admonition for the henchmen.

"So Kirsch is dead.... Well, that we must accept. He died for his country, and his emperor. But I want the truth about *why* he was killed!"

The fellow working the device gave it a couple turns; the noise it emitted this time can only be described as gruesome. My imagination had by then provided a rough sketch of the machine. It was a sort of medieval rack, with large metal spikes protruding from all its points of contact.

"Well... it ah... it seems the count he'd been working for was a spy...."

"Yes, we know that. A German spy. Kirsch was there to spy on *him*."

"I thought *you* were German spies."

"What!" He slapped me with his glove. "We are Austrians, you fool."

"Sorry. I'm not good with dialects. Well, we found some secret ciphers among the count's belongings. Perhaps Kirsch told you about those?"

"He reported nothing about ciphers. He must have been turned against us. What did these ciphers reveal?"

"Well..."

"Talk!"

The fellow operating the device punctuated his headman's directive with an even more gruesome noise.

"The count was told that the Japanese were planning an attack...."

"The Japanese are always planning an attack! Why send him here to learn about it? Why not Tsingtao, or Korea?"

"Well... According to the cipher, they're plotting an invasion of South America."

"That's fantastic!"

"It struck me that way too. But then, what do we really know about the Oriental mind?"

"True. What else?"

"The count was directed to learn the route of the invasion."

"Yes, yes, but from whom?"

"Ah, the Frenchman..."

"Dumont?"

"Yes, Captain Dumont."

"Kirsch told us he was a mere dandy."

"That was just to obscure his real mission."

"Are you saying he was a spy for the French, or the Japanese?"

"Who's to say? Perhaps both."

"A double agent! And we let him slip through our grasp.... Vienna will not be pleased."

"At least you can tell them about the Japanese invasion. Rumor has it, the Emperor is seeking El Dorado."

"Yes. I must send a dispatch at once. All right, that is enough for now."

He hurried upstairs. Shortly after, someone turned out the light that'd been shining in my face. It took some time before my eyes adjusted, but when they did, I could finally make out the fellow working the gruesome device. He was raking cinders from the furnace.

"*Bist du hungrig?*" his comrade asked him.

"*Ja.*"

They flipped a coin. I was left alone with the loser.

Luckily, Austrian thoroughness wasn't quite the same as German thoroughness. Though they'd used plenty of rope, and a Melvillian variety of knots, they'd left enough play for me to work out one of my hands. The other was then easy. When the guard went back to raking cinders, I untied my ankles. There was a coal shovel just a few yards away. I made a daring leap for it....

After landing face-first on the floor, I had another bit of luck. My captor spun around not realizing my precise whereabouts and tripped over my sprawled body. Once I'd crawled out from under him, I saw he'd hit his head on a brick pillar and was out cold.

I ran out the bulkhead and into the night. It was plenty cold, and plenty dark. I was still wearing the cashmere coat, but one of the ruthless villains had stolen my sable hat.

I crashed through the shrubbery and some minutes later found the road we arrived on. I saw no one about, so ran in the direction of town. There was a house up ahead but no sign of habitation. Then I heard an automobile leave the Austrians' residence.

In an instant, the headlights were on me. I scrambled into the woods and slid down an embankment. They'd seen me. One was scanning the scene with the car's searchlight. Another produced a lantern and followed me into the woods. I ran some ways and hid in a little patch of brush, then waited until the man with the lantern passed.

Once he'd wandered off, I crawled back up to the road. But now the car had turned around and I emerged in the glow of its headlights. I went back down the embankment and deeper into the woods. Eventually, I came upon a rustic road and headed in the direction I thought south.

It was hours before I found myself at an old mill. There, another road ran perpendicular to the one I'd been traveling. I headed up that, out of the little valley then onto a suburban stretch of Connecticut Avenue I recognized from our earlier visit. The home Sesbania shared with her parents sat just a few blocks away.

The neighborhood was dark but for a few porch lights. I found the right house and tried rousing the servants. But with their master and mistress in Europe, they must have been given the holidays off.

My feet were damp and cold, and I was on the point of exhaustion. Knowing the neighbors would be unlikely to welcome a visitor at that hour, I broke the window of the kitchen door.

Someone must have been stoking the furnace during the day, because the house was still fairly warm. I sealed the window as best I could, then went in and collapsed on a couch.

Sometime later I met the fellow who came by to stoke the furnace. I also met the policeman he'd fetched on seeing me asleep on the couch.

"It's not what it looks like," I started.

"Sure, sure," the cop said. "You just forgot your key…. Come on! Get up."

He led me out to the street car line and we rode downtown. Several times I considered offering an explanation, but by then I had trouble remembering the details myself. Ultimately, I decided pleading to house-breaking might be the course of least resistance.

It was almost nine when we got to police headquarters, and another hour before I persuaded someone to contact Lacy.

"Well, Mr. Reese. You seem to be visiting old haunts."

"Not by choice. You won't believe this, but I was abducted last night."

"Were you, now? And by who were you abducted?"

"Austrian spies..."

"I've had my fill of spies! The postmaster general complained to the commissioner. Said I was harassing his coachman. Well, let *him* deal with the spies—he'll get no help from me."

"What about me?"

"I've been thinking of that. I may be able to help you out of this fix. Put a word in with the arresting officer. In the meantime, it occurs to me this might be an advantageous time to write your record of the case of the German count."

"What? In this cell?"

"I'll have you taken to a room with a typewriter."

"But I don't have my notes."

"Too many facts would only muddle the story."

"And I can't type."

"We've a stenographer who can."

"My wife will be making inquiries. And the countess..."

"I've spoken with the countess. She thought it a fine idea."

He led me to a little room where the stenographer, colored, was waiting. Lacy explained the project to him and, after posting a guard at the door, left us alone.

At least the room was heated. I took off my shoes and stretched out on the cot which ran along one wall.

"How will you begin?" the stenographer asked.

"Are you familiar with Sherlock Holmes?"

"Reasonably."

"Well, the sergeant's looking for something heavy on the attitude and atmosphere, but light on the facts."

"That would seem contrary to the norm. Mr. Holmes is rather fond of facts."

"Well, to paraphrase Sergeant Lacy, Mr. Holmes isn't counting on a civil service pension."

"Ah. In that case, what facts can we make use of?"

"Well, you probably read about the death of the German count."

"The Count von Schnurrenberger und Kesselheim?"

"Have there been other German counts murdered recently in town?"

"Not that I'm aware of. Died of electric shock, wasn't it?"

"Electrocution." I described the contraption attached to the bureau. Then I provided him a somewhat modified cast of characters. I became Nick Carter, Emmie became the mysterious Lady McG_____, Dumont became Captain D_____, the countess became the Duchess of Alba, and Sesbania a confidence trickster well known to the New York police as Little Nell Malone. The only members of the company given their real names were Lacy and Dex Peterson. I knew neither would mind the publicity.

"Who actually committed the murder?"

"Well, Captain D_____ is safely out of the country, so let's pin it on him." I then gave him whatever else interesting I could remember, such as the coded messages; the Japanese invasion plans; the sergeant's having been knocked out after discovering Captain D____'s collection of confidential correspondence and intimate apparel; the monograph on expectoration; and, finally, Lacy's uncanny discovery of the gypsy lineage of an unnamed senator's wife. However, I left out mention of Herr Kirsch's untimely demise, my abduction, *Gamiani*, the inciting perfume, and the certain bit of anatomy I'd encountered that first night.

Some kind soul brought us coffee and doughnuts, and immediately after eating, I dozed off to the comfortingly familiar sound of the typewriter.

11

I awoke to find Lacy seated at the little desk reading the typewritten manuscript.

"Oh, you outdid yourself, Mr. Reese."

"Did I? You think the ending not too ambiguous?"

"Read that first thing. Not ambiguous at all. A secret ceremony where the Peruvian ambassador presents me with the Sacred Sash of the Order of Incas. That's one on Mr. Holmes."

"Yes, and well deserved."

"I can hardly wait to read it to the missus. Well, Mr. Reese, I guess this is good-bye. Merry Christmas to you."

"I can go?"

"The countess sent her man to drive you back."

He escorted me outside where the auto was waiting, then took my hand.

"I hope we might look forward to working another case together—and your recording of it."

"Yes, I think by the end I was getting the knack of it."

"Oh, most definitely. Well, good-bye."

I didn't exchange a single word with Thomas on the ride to the house. I wanted to convey my displeasure with his actions of the night before, though I'm not sure he glommed on to that. He whistled some perky waltz the whole way, then gave me a condescending smile when we arrived. I assume he realized he was out of the running for any Christmas tips I might be dispensing.

On my way up to take a bath, I passed the open door of the countess's study. She summoned me in.

"Where did you go off to last night?"

"Kidnapped. By Austrian spies. Seems Herr Kirsch was in their employ."

"Interesting. What did you tell them?"

"Absolutely nothing. I made my escape before they got down to the real torturing." I expected to be out of town before she'd learn differently. "Is Emmie about?"

"Out shopping, she said."

"Shopping? Didn't seem worried about me?"

"More annoyed than worried. What's going on with you two?"

"Well, she came across a perfume. A powerful feminine aphrodisiac."

"*Deux nuits d'excès?*"

"Yes. That's the one."

"I think I know how she came by that."

"You do?"

"Someone's been having fun with the presents under the tree. That was meant for me.... No matter, I've been through the experience. But why would a powerful feminine aphrodisiac cause you problems?"

"Well, last night was *nuit deux*. And she'd been reading a book.... *Gamiani*.... I think she had plans."

"And you assume she gave them up simply because you skipped out?"

"Skipped out?"

"Yes. How foolish of you."

"If you remember, I was out performing a commission for you. And I had missed *nuit une* as well, and for the same reason."

"Are you trying to blame me?"

"Merely pointing out it wasn't by choice. I suppose you wouldn't know if last night..."

"Don't you trust your wife, Harry?"

"That depends what you mean by trust. Yesterday morning when I came into the room, Geneviève was there... and they both were looking... disheveled."

"Oh.... Well, just be glad I don't have a dog."

"Dog?"

"Have you read the book?"

"Only the first episode."

"Well, then you have something to look forward to."

"I see." Next Christmas, Emmie would be getting a new ribbon for her typewriter. "When did she expect to be home?"

"She's not coming directly here. We've been invited to a gathering at the Belgian Embassy."

"How should I dress?"

"When I say we, I mean Emmie, Sesbania, and myself. I'm afraid you weren't asked. There'll be a reception, then we'll go caroling at some of the other embassies. At midnight, there's a mass at the Franciscan monastery, then it's back to the Belgians' for a late supper."

"I see. Well, Merry Christmas."

"*Oh, please*.... And shut the door on your way out."

The itinerary she had outlined struck me as somewhat anomalous. I found it difficult to imagine her ladyship traipsing about on a cold night crooning on about men's goodwill toward men. And if I were those Franciscans, I'd count the chalices before letting anyone out the door.

I ate alone in the dining room, reading the newspaper. It was filled with the sort of insipid tripe that makes you feel particularly small if you're spending Christmas Eve alone. Meanwhile, I could hear the servants having a jolly time in the kitchen.

By the time I'd finished examining the dessert for chicken bones, I'd lost my appetite. I went into the billiard room and absentmindedly practiced shots while putting away a generous quantity of the countess's finest brandy. It must have been past midnight when Geneviève entered the room. There was a look in her eyes. And she bore a distinctive scent....

"You're wearing the perfume...."

"Yes, Mrs. Reese must have given me what remained of hers. It was left in my room.... I wanted to ask... Is there anything else you might... need? ...Anything?"

"Ah..."

"It was cruel the way you were left alone, on Christmas Eve.... And now I too..."

"Isn't Gustave about?"

"Collapsed in bed, drunk! Dreaming of his rich young widow..."

Personally, I couldn't blame the fellow. There's something about rich young widows that sets a man to dreaming. But I wondered if even the dreamiest rendering could replicate the inferno then playing in the maid's eyes.

"And Thomas?"

"Thomas! *The loyal manservant*..." I doubt the phrase was ever before spoken with such obvious contempt. "He cares for no woman but *her!*" An unmistakable fervency had entered her voice, something I'd not noted in our previous conversations. "Why should either of us be alone?"

I believe her question was a rhetorical one, but by now her arms were wrapped about my waist and a response of one sort or another seemed unavoidable.

"Care for a game?"

"A game!" She pulled back from me. "You think I came in here to play billiards?"

"Well, what if I give you odds?" I held out a cue, but she indicated that she preferred another....

~~~~~

At four in the afternoon on Christmas Day, we boarded the Congressional Limited for New York and what promised to be anything but a sentimental journey. Emmie hadn't spoken much that day and I'd thought it advisable to follow her lead. While she pretended to be reading Thackeray, I pretended to be reading Conan Doyle.

No one in the house had risen until well after noon, and Christmas dinner was a decidedly somber affair. Even Sesbania appeared subdued. She'd opened her presents on their return to the house, which must have been after three that morning. Her excited yelps had helpfully announced their arrival. I came down and was surprised to find a gift for myself from the countess—less so when I realized the promisingly large box held nothing beyond two return tickets to New York.

By the time we went to the dining car for a light supper, Emmie had thawed a bit. I'd mistaken her mood as anger with me, but it gradually became clear it had more to do with the countess having once again toyed with her.

In an effort to divert her, I began describing my misadventures of the last few days—the frigid crossing of the creek, my abduction and escape, and finally my discovery after breaking into Sesbania's house. This cheered her up some. But I'd saved the best part for last: the disposing of Herr Kirsch's body in the canal. By then, Emmie and I'd had numerous adventures involving corpses in canals. However, this was the first in which either of us had a hand in the launching of the body.

"It was almost exactly where we came across that drunken Irishman five years ago," I told her.

"I can't believe you didn't take me along."

"It wasn't something I had any choice about. I'd have been happy to trade places with you," I said, only afterward remembering with whom she'd spent those early-morning hours.

She blushed, then changed the subject to the murder of the count. "What did Lacy actually learn?"

"Next to nothing—apart from the Japanese invasion plans."

She smiled. "That was my idea. And the French plans for Vauxhall."

I pretended to be surprised.

"Who do you think committed the murder?" she asked.

"Well, I'd wager Dumont set up the device."

"Yes, that much is obvious. But you realize..."

"That someone put him up to it? A woman, perhaps?"

"Why are you looking at me like that?"

"I was taking stock. Your lips do have a lubricious quality, and you can't deny your eyes have been looking a little languid of late."

"What are you talking about?"

"Just waxing poetic." I doubted she knew nothing about the forged letters, but I saw no point in confronting her with my suspicions. Emmie may not be a master of deceit, but she is a seasoned journeyman. "Are you implying you don't know the identity of the woman behind it?"

"Not at all. You met her yourself, on Sunday."

"Mrs. Quinlan? How do you know about her?" I asked.

"The countess. Apparently, she knew that the lady was in correspondence with the count. And the night he was killed, Thomas drove her home after replacing the fuse."

"Well, I suppose that makes some sense."

"Why did you word your question like that?"

"Like what?"

"You said, 'How do you know about her?' It makes it sound as if you already knew something about Mrs. Quinlan yourself."

"What would I know about a gypsy princess?" The strained attempt at a witticism only heightened her curiosity. My forehead had become uncomfortably moist. I took a handkerchief from my pocket.

Emmie stared at it as I mopped my brow, then reached over and took it from my hand. It wasn't a hand-kerchief at all. It was the unidentified lady's undergarment I'd filched from Dumont's collection. She brought it to her nose. It must have shared a pocket with the perfume Mrs. Quinlan had given me.

"I suppose you'll tell me you'd planned to give me this for Christmas as well?"

"Yes, but with one thing and another..."

She examined the thing from every possible angle; by her expression, I suspect she found its precise function as much a mystery as I did. Not so the smart young couple then passing our table. Two sets of eyebrows rose in unison and the lady had to bite her lip to avert an involuntary titter. Her giddy escort wasn't so inhibited. Emmie smiled back at them and slipped it into her bag.

It seemed an opportune time to shift the conversation elsewhere.

"Tell me, who was it then who knocked out Lacy?" I asked.

"I assume it was Thomas, acting on orders."

"The countess wanted the money?"

"I can't say definitively, but she is very fond of the stuff."

We drank a second bottle of wine and disembarked in a warm Christmas glow. Emmie uncharacteristically insisted I give a coin to each of the panhandlers we passed and the beneficent mood continued even after our arrival at our apartment in Brooklyn. The maid was hosting an impromptu celebration of the holiday with three comely friends, six British sailors, and the last of our liquor supply. They weren't the least bit upset at our breaking in on them—even took the time to teach us some fascinating sea chanteys.

We slept well into the next afternoon, even relegated as we were to the second-best bed. Emmie had agreed that it might seem inhospitable to confront the stoker occupying ours while he was busy. She also agreed that our next maid should be French. Now that I think of it, the suggestion originated with her.

It had been a fairly typical case, as my cases go— meaning there was nothing remotely typical about it. True, there'd been the requisite two murders. Yet no one was likely to be brought to justice for either.

I can't claim that troubled me too terribly. The more one is exposed to what passes for justice, the less enthralled with it one becomes. Besides, one could argue that while Kirsch may not have deserved a death sentence for his opinion of Gustave's strudel, he might well have gotten one anyway for espionage.

As for the count, it was never entirely clear that the device Dumont created was intended to kill him. The Frenchman seemed genuinely surprised when the word electrocution was introduced the morning of the aristocrat's death.

I would say the most singular aspect of this case, as Dr. Watson would phrase it, was its opacity. I'm used to gleaning only a fraction of what goes on—particularly where Emmie is involved—but never has it been quite so small a fraction. I couldn't even be sure that the cook killed Kirsch, or that Dumont created the device behind the count's bureau.

The dissembling this time had come too thick and too fast to be the work of a lone perpetrator. Many hands must have played their parts. Still, I had little doubt there was one mastermind behind it all.

Part II

Sesbania's Version of Events

To my dear husband, to be read on the eve of our wedding...

It's difficult to write this to a man I likely have never set eyes upon, as I doubt you are quite the ideal I imagine you now, just five weeks shy of my seventeenth birthday. I can only hope any difference derives from an evolution in my tastes, and not from any lowering of standards. But regardless, I must take it on faith that my future self has at least judged one thing correctly: you'll do.

And yet, a doubt lingers. What if she *hasn't* judged correctly? What if—blinded by a handsome physique, or, more to be feared, an irascible charm—she has laid herself open to all the myriad injuries a husband might inflict upon a wife? Why, then, shouldn't some precaution be taken now? Mustn't we expend all conceivable efforts to forestall tragedy? And, more to the point, isn't it only fair that you be warned?

Indeed so, I say. And that, dear husband, is the very crux of my letter: to make clear, beyond all doubt, just what your blushing bride is capable of.

The events here described took place some years previous to my recording of them, but be assured, they are still fresh in my mind. The idea of setting them down, and in a letter addressed to you, originated with a woman you might call my mentor. A woman who herself had some trouble with a husband—if only briefly.

One last point before I begin the account proper: do be sure to read this chronicle in its entirety. I know that it is long, and your anticipation, I hope, great. Nonetheless, forewarned is forearmed....

1

Clever—that was the word used most often to describe me in that tranquil period between childhood and adolescence. It is a wonderfully supple word. Speakers could rest confident my doting parents would interpret the remark as a compliment to my intelligence. But more often than not, it was my impish cunning on which they were remarking; and they meant no compliment.

I'm sure you have already deduced that I was hopelessly spoiled as a child. I know I exhibit all the faults which accompany the condition, and I have reason to doubt that I shall develop the will, or the character, to shed them between now and our inevitable introduction. Of one thing I'm certain, however: you are under no delusion that you will be my corrector. For the very thought of tying myself to a Mr. Knightley, a living testament to all that is good and proper, *makes me ill.*

My father, being a lawyer and therefore himself no prisoner of ethics, saw my proclivities in a purely positive light. Of course he could not say so. When I outwitted my governess, or convinced the child next door to surrender to me for safekeeping the silver dollar she'd just received, he would admonish me in his most serious tone. And, as often as not, he'd manage to turn away before the glow of paternal pride undermined the reproach.

Mother was equally to blame. My father has always insisted he won her in a card game in the Argentine and she has never contradicted his account. But that may just be her nature; Mother would gladly sacrifice her reputation for the sake of an amusing story. She is the most relentlessly unserious person I have ever met.

Adults often find her trying, but both Father and I revel in her unreal world. For him, I suspect, it offers a welcome relief from the sordid realm of money and politics he labors in. For me, it is the land of my birth and I've known no other—a land where an only child may be indulged unchecked.

You can imagine the problem this presented for the alien adult tasked with my education. School, of any sort, was out of the question. I believe three were tried, none lasting more than a few days. Fortunately, my father's practice was lucrative enough to allow for the hiring of a governess. We all three thought this the ideal solution. The governesses themselves, however, were not always of the same opinion.

Some lasted as long as a year—most, no more than a month or two. Then, late in my eleventh year, Father brought home Miss Ditka. She was Bulgarian—a member of a disqualified branch of the royal family, she told us. It may have been true, of course. But one met so few Bulgarians in our neighborhood that there was nobody in a position to challenge her claim.

She spoke French, German, and Russian fluently, Spanish reasonably, and English haltingly—a slight inconvenience more than compensated for by her utter imperturbability. She cared less about mathematics than I did, and held nothing but the utmost scorn for science. "The genius Newton," she would say, "he saw an apple fall from a tree. Who hasn't seen an apple fall from a tree!" It was not a question I felt either inclined or equipped to debate.

Mostly, we read novels, while she smoked cigarette

after cigarette in an endless stream. If my mother asked what we were working on that day, Miss Ditka would give her a detailed summation in either French or German, languages to Mother incomprehensible.

Miss Ditka's one indisputable talent, and the principal reason I have injected her into my account, was penmanship. She had the most elegant hand I've ever encountered. Mother would ask her to make out all her invitations, not even minding—or perhaps not noticing—the unique diction and inventive orthography. I spent nearly an hour every day trying to mimic my tutor's lovely script, partly to humor my mother, but partly for my own purposes.

When we were alone, Miss Ditka often dropped hints of her past. I imagine she thought there was little danger in a girl my age grasping the implications of a comment such as, "A woman without friends cannot be bound by scruples—and a woman should never depend on friends." I need hardly tell you what effect this had on me. A few years before, my literary taste ran no further than *The Wonderful Wizard of Oz*. Now I was reading Gothic novels under the guidance of a Balkan princess who spoke in epigrams.

I became obsessed with this beguiling tutor's past life. But she steadfastly refused to divulge details, no matter how annoying I made myself. (And you may believe, I had a unique faculty for annoying adults.) Thus thwarted, I took matters into my own little hands.

I'd been given a diary for my birthday and had yet to make use of it. Not due to any lack of vanity, but merely out of laziness. I began by dating the first entry seven years before, and adding beside it, "The Palace, Sophia."

What followed was an elaborate tale of intrigue, lust,

and betrayal, or, at any rate, intrigue, lust, and betrayal as understood by a precocious eleven-year-old schooled by a Slavic princess. And it was all in a hand nearly identical to Miss Ditka's own.

When I had finished several months' worth of narrative, I showed it to her. It would be difficult to describe how genuinely pleased she was. I had flattered both her pedagogical prowess and her narcissism. "What a dangerous little forger you will be...," she said.

It wasn't until some months later that I was able to decide whether her comment was meant as accolade or accusation. By then Miss Ditka had left us, on mutually amicable terms. Amicable, at least, until certain checks began showing up at my father's bank. Not only had she mastered his signature, but she knew to add just enough variation to make her work convincing.

It wasn't long after my creation of the princess's personal diary that a new obsession took hold. This was in the fall of 1906. We had a cook who was rather preoccupied with the more sordid crimes recounted in the newspapers. These were not the sorts of things my mother would discuss, so the cook, Jessie, would share them with me. Her renditions dwelt heavily on the more gruesome features of the crimes and so provided a useful supplement to the Gothic novels, which all too often were squeamish about such things. In time, I took to reading her the stories from the newspaper while she prepared dinner.

In November of that year, the trial of Chester Gillette began in a small village in New York state. Gillette had been courting a young woman employed, like him, in his uncle's skirt factory. That summer, he had coaxed this fresh innocent up to a small lake in the Adirondacks. And there she drowned—under *very* suspicious circumstances.

Gillette denied culpability, but Jessie and I had no doubts. "He'd ruined the girl," she told me. "You wait and see." At that moment, I had only the haziest idea what was meant by ruining a girl. But by the time the verdict came down in early December, my conception was not nearly so hazy. Jessie was not timid when speaking of such topics and I later confirmed much of what she told me by reading *Sexology*, a book authored by a Professor Walling which I found hidden in my mother's closet. Though perhaps confirm is too strong a word, as the good professor spoke of anatomy almost as elliptically as the authors of my Gothic novels. He did, however, explain the general course of pregnancy.

Jessie held a low opinion of men generally. But men who wronged women, in any degree, she held in the greatest contempt. My good-natured father usually passed muster. But that didn't mean she wasn't ever-vigilant. I remember once, when confronted with some no doubt illogical stance of my mother, he raised his voice in frustration. Jessie happened to be in the room delivering a roast. She dropped the platter onto the table—the clatter effectively cutting my father short. In the fall, the carving knife had slid off the platter. She picked it up from the table and held it for a moment while turning a gaze upon my father which mixed equal parts derision and menace. Her point taken, she set down the knife and quietly left the room. Conversation was subdued for the remainder of the meal.

I don't think I can possibly convey the effect the episode had on my thinking. Especially coming as it did so recently after the discovery of my mother's book, in which the author describes most women's wedding nights as scenes of horror, due to the incompetence and selfishness of their mates. (The professor made a woman's pleasure something of a cause, though he was exasperatingly scant on details. And I can say now with some authority he was mistaken when in a condemnatory discussion of onanism he states that a woman cannot realize her entitled pleasure without seminal fluid being in contact with the neck of the womb. In fact, his readers would have been better served if his extended attacks on self-fulfillment had been left out of the book entirely.)

I need hardly tell you, there was much joy in the kitchen when the murderous Gillette was found guilty that first week of December.

"Now, he'll get his!"

"Will they hang him?" I asked.

"Electrocution! Fried up like an egg on a griddle! Oh, what I wouldn't give to see that."

Jessie was proved right when Gillette was sentenced on the tenth. She then went with me to the library, where we devoured all that was available on the subject of human electrocution. I suggested to Father that providing her fare to the place of execution as a Christmas present might return him to her good graces, but he correctly anticipated an appeal.

This unwarranted delay annoyed Jessie and me to no end. But welcome diversion was close at hand. A new case of wronged womanhood appeared in the newspaper just as the Gillette trial was coming to a conclusion. Better still, this was a local one: a Mrs. Bradley shot and killed a former senator from Utah named Brown at his Washington hotel. Over the coming days, ever more details emerged which quickly made clear the lady's motivation. It seems the ex-senator had fathered two children by Mrs. Bradley, and yet he refused to marry the poor woman!

When it appeared that charges would be brought against the plucky divorcée, I honestly feared Jessie would take the carving knife and settle the matter with the pig-headed prosecutor herself. It was Father who suggested we instead focus our energies on raising funds for Mrs. Bradley's defense. He put in the first dollar, and—on realizing his contribution had not impressed the mercurial cook—the next twenty as well.

Some months before then, my parents had made plans for the three of us to take a European vacation over the holidays. Though I'd been excited at the prospect, I now felt torn. Jessie was going to her brother's home in Baltimore and there would be no one to carry on the important work on behalf of Mrs. Bradley. After a good deal of soul-searching, I informed my parents I would remain behind.

I must confess, I was more than a little surprised when they almost too quickly acquiesced to my plan. I had anticipated various arguments against it, and prepared noble little orations countering each of them. One of the finest—and the one I expected to conclude with— ended with me so drained by the verbal sparring that I grudgingly agreed to make the trip. But no sooner had I tendered my proposal than they acceded. That same evening, Father phoned a family friend who invited me to stay with her.

2

The home of the Countess von Schnurrenberger und Kesselheim was located just above Dupont Circle in the neighborhood called Kalorama Heights. It was, both in its furnishings and in its operation, a far more formal house than our own. But I savored my every visit. As any reader of novels knows, formality is often just a facade hiding dark secrets. And I have always been partial to secrets, the darker the better.

In spite of her grand title, the countess, as everyone called her, was not of royal blood, nor even German. She acquired the name on marrying the then current count several years earlier. Not long afterward, he died as the result of what she referred to as an unavoidable accident. I believe what she meant by unavoidable was that he had no reason to suspect his Charlotte Russe had been seasoned with a chicken bone.

Strictly speaking, on the ascension of the late count's nephew to the title, the countess became the *Dowager* Countess von Schnurrenberger und Kesselheim, a repellent appellation, particularly for a woman still in the bloom of youth. Flouting the traditions of nobility, she simply declined the emendation—a remarkable choice in a city which made a religion of protocol. Interestingly, not one among her acquaintances, so far as I am aware, chose to point out the discrepancy. Perhaps because she entertained so liberally, and soft desserts mask so wonderfully.

On the twelfth of December, the countess's manservant, Thomas, drove us to the station. I exchanged good-byes with Mother and Father and then accompanied Thomas back to the house in Kalorama.

As I mentioned, I always relished my visits, but especially so now, without my parents. The countess was nearly as indulgent of me as they were themselves. But in a very different way. My mother and I communicated as children. The countess treated children as she did adults and expected them to act accordingly. I don't mean that she was strict, only that excited exclamations, silly giggling, and loud play annoyed her. What's more, she lived very much in the real world and had little use for the fantasies which comprised so much of the time spent with my mother.

The countess was—or I should say, is—the most accomplished of women, witty, cultured, and charming. At least, when she chooses to be. Not classically beautiful, but with a unique allure all her own. If I described her features, I've little doubt you would find them lacking. But if you spent a single evening with her, you would never forget the experience.

It is on her advice that I am writing this now. She tells me that the sort of trouble she had with her late husband—albeit fleetingly—can be quite easily avoided, *provided* a husband is sensitive to the feelings of his wife, *and* suffers no delusions regarding just what she is capable of.

That very first evening the countess was holding a dinner party for some important people, senators and whatnot. She suggested that I would probably prefer to eat earlier with the servants. Headstrong though I was, I had learned by then that whenever the countess suggests one might prefer one thing over another, the wise girl aligns her preferences with the suggestion. In this case, she made the choice easier by assigning me the mission of spying on the servants, a commission I welcomed wholeheartedly.

I had known Thomas since he was in service to the countess during her residence at the German Embassy. We were often left in each other's company during the countess's visits to my parents and I had become by then something of a confidante. I believe he saw me as the one person he could share his frustrations with vis à vis the countess. It was no secret that he adored the woman, and I don't mean solely in the manner a loyal retainer adores his benevolent mistress. It was a genuine passion. Whether it was ever consummated, I can only guess. The countess went through lovers at a rather torrid pace and there may have been a time, or times, when she was in need of someone handy. And handy he was, apparently. Once I observed him giving her ladyship a foot massage, and the effect it had on me dwarfed that of the Gothic novels, Dr. Walling's *Sexology*, and the most sordid newspaper accounts combined. It seemed to work on the countess with similar efficacy. I resolved then and there that any husband of mine would be required to master the art. Please make a mental note of that now. If we are lucky, Thomas is still alive and willing to take on an apprentice.

Gustave, the cook, I had also known for some time. He spoke only French—unless he felt inclined to do otherwise. He was under the misapprehension that I was a blameless child and treated me accordingly, even making me cute little pastries shaped like animals, and not seeming to mind the delight I took in dismembering the insipid creatures.

The maid, Geneviève, was new and regarded me much the same as Gustave. When I told her I'd had a governess who was a Bulgarian princess, she seemed not a bit surprised, then said something to me in that language. Unfortunately, Miss Ditka had never taught me a word of her native tongue. But even at that young age, I knew there was something curious about a maid who professed to have grown up in Paris being acquainted with the language of a distant Balkan state.

Also there was Herr Kirsch, the then current count's valet. He was not an ugly man, but neither would I have called him handsome. And his disposition fell on the far side of pleasant. He had the German formality of Thomas, but lacked Thomas's gentleness. Nonetheless, he alone of the three men held Geneviève's interest. She was always flirting with him—subtly, but unmistakably. I found this as suspicious as her knowledge of Bulgarian. Yes, Geneviève had secrets....

Sometime after the countess's guests had finished dining, and well after I was supposed to be in bed, I came upon the maid listening at the door of the billiard room.

"Boo!" I said.

I'd learned long before that nothing was quite so amusing as an adult caught by a child doing something illicit. They will attempt every excuse imaginable, thinking one or another will certainly work on the unformed being before them.

"I thought I heard someone call for me...."

"And you just wanted to be sure before you interrupted," I helpfully added.

"Yes.... But I must have misunderstood."

"It's these *damn* oak doors. Why need they be so thick? We have the same problem at our house."

I went off, leaving Geneviève with her mouth agape. Whether it was the unexpected profanity which left her speechless, or my familiarity with the complications faced by the eavesdropper, I cannot say.

The next morning, after our breakfast but still some hours before the countess was likely to make her appearance, Thomas asked if I would accompany him into town. He needed to run some errands for the countess in the automobile. As soon as we pulled away from the house, he began fulminating about the other house guests. There were three, two men and a woman.

The first was the new count, successor to my hostess's husband. He was a handsome man, elegant and suave. He kissed my hand and complimented my clumsy German. He was a charmer, all right. He'd been by then at the house for most of three months. Thomas said he had fallen hopelessly in love with the countess, but that she had tired of him. Thomas despised the count, but since he'd lost the affection of the countess, he saw him more as an annoyance than a threat.

Not so Captain Dumont. He was a young French officer. Blond, bright, and as quick-witted as the countess herself. He was an assistant attaché at the embassy. There hadn't been space for him there, so he'd been boarding at a hotel. Soon after their meeting, the countess invited him to stay with her. Thomas had hoped her motivation was simply to get rid of the count. But now he harbored doubts.

The third guest was a writer. I had met her, briefly, several years before. Her position in the house was complex, according to Thomas. Apparently, the countess had led her to believe she would be divulging the details of her fascinating life. Did I mention that, prior to marrying the former count, she had for some time operated as an international jewel thief? So successful was she, she'd had her own pseudo-anonymous moniker: Madame B_____. How I would love to achieve that level of notoriety! Just please tell me I haven't married a Patterson or a Phillips—I don't think I could bear being Madame P_____.

I'm afraid I've strayed some from the story. As I said, this woman author, Emily Reese—or Emmie, as she was often, nauseatingly, called (I hope I may assume the use of such diminutives for adults makes you as ill as it does me)—was under the impression she was there to write the countess's biography. In fact, she was there to divert the attentions of the count.

At this, she was a failure. She was a shameless self-promoter, whose main concern was finding someone—anyone—willing to read one of her literary efforts, the manuscripts of which she carried in her luggage. Unfortunately, the count was the sort of aristocrat who took a dim view of ambition generally, and in women particularly. But I shouldn't be too hard on the authoress. She could be witty, and was one of the few people able to stand her ground with the countess *and* remain in her good graces. Under the pretense of self-deprecation, she matched her hostess dig for dig. Luckily for her, the countess found her amusing. And so did Captain Dumont. But the count did not.

On the way home from our errands, I swore a solemn oath to Thomas that I would rid him of the twin menaces: the count and the French captain. I can't really claim I acted solely out of sympathy for his plight. To me, it was something of a game, a challenge, and a test of my cunning.

The captain was the most immediate threat, holding as he then did the countess's affections. That same morning, I formulated a plan to arouse a romance between him and Mrs. Reese, or, failing in that, at least inspire a suspicion in the mind of the countess. But first, I needed to gain a sample of each of the parties' handwriting.

I approached the authoress in her room and asked if I might be permitted to read one of her manuscripts. She told me she feared they might not be appropriate for a child my age. Needless to say, I now became exceedingly interested in them. Overcoming locked drawers is child's play for children such as me and by dinner time I had abstracted her bizarre and vaguely graphic account of a boy who runs away with the circus while undergoing his sexual awakening. Though arresting reading, it fell short of my expectations in two respects: the poor protagonist never achieves satisfaction, and it was typewritten. Later, however, while she was out for the evening, I returned to her room and found several pages of correspondence. It was rather dull stuff, groveling letters she planned to send to various Washington litterateurs, but more than adequate for my purposes.

Now came the actual composing of the billets-doux. At this, my experience was rather limited, and I felt sure the oblique language of the Gothic novels too plodding and imprecise. I needed some authentic matter to work from. I thought the French maid a likely candidate, given her obvious interest in the count's valet.

I ventured up to Herr Kirsch's third-floor room, hoping Geneviève had already initiated a correspondence. The room was curiously lacking in personal items—no photographs, no letters, no papers of any sort.

Geneviève's room was just one door down. I hoped

she might have a diary, or, better still, a draft of a love letter in progress. I did find some correspondence, but nothing of the sort I needed, and nothing else of interest—well, save some revealingly fashioned wooden tools which I took at the time for aids in the darning of socks. They weren't the usual gourd-shaped eggs, but cylindrical, with a slight curve to them and a tapering tip. And they were worn remarkably smooth. Evidence, I assumed, of the diligence with which she went at it.

3

The very next morning, luck came my way in the form of Gustave's pocketbook. He'd left it unattended on the kitchen table. This was a large, flat wallet in which he kept all sorts of papers: recipes, menus, shopping lists, and, most providentially, love notes from a thoroughly uninhibited lady who called herself Gwenie. So fiery were these missives—and, I might add, so detailed—I willingly forgave the woman her ridiculous name.

All I needed to do now was recompose Gwenie's evocative letters in Mrs. Reese's quite conventional hand. I chose the three I considered most auspicious. I based this judgment on how many euphemisms strained my comprehension, the acme being so cloudy as to be downright milky: ...*my insatiable, gaping maw of passion, aflood in a bubbling river of Aphrodite's rich drippings....*

I would have thought the meaning of such passages was lost on Gustave as well, his English being at best rudimentary. But perhaps reading between the lines was enough for a Frenchman, especially when the pages came tacky to the touch.

Since Mrs. Reese was herself conversant in French, I set to work rendering Gwenie's letters in that tongue. But on reading the results, I feared the combination of her saucy prose and my too-literal translations sounded more like a serialized portrayal of feeding time at the zoo than a testament of mad love. It seemed wisest to leave the text in its pure native state. One does not easily adjust genius. Nevertheless, I kept my translations and they later came in useful.

I chose for the first message to Captain Dumont the tamest of my prototypes. After all, one can't simply jump in with the gaping maw of passion without first laying the foundation. (Have you ever noticed that once sexual allusions are introduced, you begin to see them everywhere?) By lunch time, the letter written in Mrs. Reese's hand was ready. I slipped it under the captain's door.

When I learned that he wasn't expected back until dinner, I initiated a second avenue of attack. As every good Christian girl knows, idle hands are the devil's workshop. (There's another!) Having seen Mrs. Reese's home address among her correspondence, I took the liberty of sending an anonymous letter to her husband warning him that his wife was slipping, and slipping fast. I used for this my own script, which had by then the appearance of that of a lady of some breeding.

Eventually, the captain returned and went into his room. My own room was just opposite his and I posted myself at the half-opened door awaiting developments. I'm not sure what exactly I expected to happen, but certainly something. At that moment, Mrs. Reese could be heard typing in her room and the captain might easily approach her chamber unobserved. Instead, he sauntered downstairs to the billiard room. I watched through the keyhole as he poured himself a whiskey, then bounced the balls about the table. I wondered if I had erred in my choice of letters.

After we in the kitchen had eaten, and the others had sat down in the dining room, I positioned myself in the front hall. There was a cushioned bench there and I knew from prior experience that there was just enough space beside it for me to place a cushion on the floor and then wedge my body in place. From there, I could hear all that went on in the dining room. My view of the diners, however, was impeded by the table itself. But in the event, this below-deck vista proved to be just what was needed.

The countess, the captain, and Mrs. Reese carried on a lively conversation in French and English, while the count mostly sulked. I thought I detected something suggestive in several of the captain's comments to Mrs. Reese, but he was such a relentless flirt, I couldn't with certainty ascribe this to my efforts. Then I noticed his foot. The table was quite large and the four of them were all seated near the far end, the countess at the head, the two men on either side of her, and Mrs. Reese beside the count. I assumed the arrangement was chosen by their hostess.

The captain was a tall man, but not so long-legged that his foot could reach all the way to Mrs. Reese. Still, he sent several forays in that direction—hoping, I suspect, she would meet him halfway. I realized then it was a mistake not to have made the amorous communication bidirectional. But the captain had not given up. He made some exaggerated flurry with his fork while telling a story involving a woman I now believe was a courtesan of some French politician, but then took to be his laundress. Such are the nuances of language.

Under the pretense of a dramatic gesture, he sent the fork flying over the table. Then, laughing apologies, he hurried around to retrieve it. It had landed with strategic precision, mere inches from Mrs. Reese's chair. He bent down upon a knee, and while his right hand retrieved the fork, his left gave the lady's calf a brief massage.

I imagine at the more sophisticated tables of Europe, a woman knows how to maintain her composure while a man is subtly exploring beneath her skirt. Not so Mrs. Reese. There was an audible inhalation. I could not see her expression, but while she sat frozen, both the count and the countess dropped their silver and went silent.

The captain returned to his seat holding up the fork triumphantly and attempting to plaster over his faux pas with an impish apology. The results could not be termed a success. The countess made a noise which those unfamiliar with her might have interpreted as a muffled laugh. I don't think a single one of us then in attendance were under any such misconception.

Later, Thomas and I conferred.

"You did well," he told me. "The countess could barely hide her anger."

Apparently, he had his own blind for spying on the dinner table.

"Yes, but what we need is some correspondence *from* the captain *to* Mrs. Reese. I don't suppose he writes to the countess?"

"He does. You want to see those letters?"

"Oh, they'd be wonderfully convincing."

"We must be very careful. If the countess were to learn of it...."

"I don't see how she would. Certainly, Mrs. Reese won't be revealing them."

I was somewhat surprised at the audacity of his plan. That evening, when the countess and her three guests went off to a recital at the Russian Embassy, Thomas took me into her study. How he knew I would be able to pick the lock of her desk, I can't say. But pick it I did. We found three letters from Captain Dumont, and one from the count. They were all in French.

I began at once making copies and had only just finished and replaced the originals when the countess returned with her party.

I spent most of the next morning translating these letters with the help of the countess's French dictionary. Concurrent with these literary endeavors, I continued my efforts on behalf of Mrs. Bradley. I found it awkward asking the servants to contribute, but not so awkward as they would have found it to refuse a protégée of the countess's. Mrs. Reese gave me a dollar and the countess five, though I considered those merely initial installments. A vague hint that I knew *something* about *something* proved to be just the sort of prod needed to impel the captain to contribute. Each time we passed, he would salute, shout "*Fraternité!*" and give me a franc.

The count, on the other hand, contributed one single dime and suggested I use it to buy candy for myself, rather than in promoting the cause of an assassin. I politely thanked him for his advice, then gave him an open invitation to dinner at our house. The day before at lunch I had witnessed him devour a plate of mushrooms. Jessie, you see, had grown up in the country. She knew all there was to know about the culinary fungi—*and* their equally useful cousins, the toadstools.

That evening, Saturday, the countess was to give a large dinner party. The guest list included several congressmen and senators, so I knew before they even arrived it would be a dull affair. Father often needed to entertain such men and it always disgusted me to see him demean himself by flattering his inferiors. Their wives were generally not much better, but in that evening's haul was a Mrs. Quinlan, the young, attractive wife of a much older (and, I assume, much wealthier) senator.

Mrs. Quinlan's other attributes were unremarkable—save one. While nearly all women were charmed by the suave count, she was thoroughly captivated. When he slid in close, she did likewise—hanging on his every word, as he droned endlessly on about Goethe's immortality and other such nonsense. When she asked to run her fingers along his dueling scar, I knew I had my girl.

I slipped upstairs and immediately began a new transcription of Gwenie's correspondence. For this edition, I used a loopy, girlish script, even changing the dots to circles. I addressed the first letter to "My dear Count," and signed it, "Mrs. Q." The salutation of the second ran warmer: "My light, of this long winter night," and the signature I made an illegible scrawl—I'd unfortunately not caught the lady's Christian name. The third began, "Sword of my sheath,"—I took it as a given the count knew his Latin. This one I signed with an impression of my damp lips, colored discreetly with a drop of my own blood. (It's only too easy for a young girl to get carried away with these things.)

I was fast asleep long before the evening broke up, but consequently rose long before the rest of the house. I made my way into the upstairs servants' hall and from there into the count's bedroom. The door creaked awfully, but the count gave no indication of waking. I saw the suit he'd been wearing on a stand just inside the door and slipped the first of the letters in a pocket. (Later, I made sure that all the doors in the house were adequately oiled.)

From that moment, I had not a second's rest until Christmas. I slipped a copy of Captain Dumont's letter to the countess under the door of "Emily, *ma chérie*," then prepared another envelope for her husband. In this, I included the French version of Gwenie's first letter, addressed to "*Cher capitaine, mon capitaine*," and signed, "*À toi pour toujours,* Emmie"; a copy of the phony I'd just slipped under the woman's door; and, when it occurred to me Mr. Reese might not be able to read French, English versions of each. It won't surprise you, I'm sure, that my hand was already developing a cramp.

That next day, while the captain was out, a letter addressed to him arrived in the morning mail. It was from Paris, and in a woman's hand. Thomas and I took it up to my room, and there, under his tutelage, I removed the wax seal undamaged.

It was in French, of course, and it took some time before I had it all translated. Apparently, there had been an understanding between this girl and the captain, or at least an assumption on her part that they were to have been wedded sometime the previous fall. She understood, she said, that his duties must be attended to, and assured him she would await his return patiently. The rest of the letter dwelt on the mundane and was written in a style unlikely to induce a young cavalier such as the captain to hurry home and surrender the independence he so obviously enjoyed. But she did, with her references to chateaux, operas, and biscuit factories, make one thing amply clear. Her family was well-off. Very well-off.

As much as her limp disposition wearied me, I took it upon myself to come to this weak sister's aid. First, I destroyed the photograph she had included. If it was anything like an accurate rendition, her chances could only be improved by betting on the unreliability of the captain's memory.

In the recomposed letter—written, naturally, in her hand—she longed for him so thoroughly her body ached. She feared that if left unsated, her hunger would grow into a wild passion, and devotion to any one man become an impossibility. So much for the enticement, now for the prod.

She alluded to a suitor her father hoped she would marry. He was slightly older than the captain, but taller, and quite wealthy in his own right. Of course, she would wait for the captain, or, at any rate, try to. Oh, but how her every inch yearned for masculine attention, how her being begged for completion—the completion which only a man can provide a woman.

Thomas, at least, was most impressed. So much so, he ponied up a further seventy-five cents for Mrs. Bradley's fund. He told me he had stolen it from the count. I had no particular reason to doubt his account, but I did suspect he may have confessed to the crime simply because he knew it would please me.

4

When the countess mentioned at lunch that Mrs. Quinlan would be coming for coffee that afternoon, the count and I were both at pains to cloak our enthusiastic interest. Dame Fortune was smiling upon us.

As soon as I left the table, I sought out my copy of the count's missive to the countess. I hoped to use this as a template for a love note to Mrs. Quinlan. But that proved an impossibility. First, it was in French, a language I couldn't be sure the lady understood. Second, and more critically, it was as lifeless as the letter from Captain Dumont's fiancée. I therefore decided to write one from scratch, using some of the captain's more poetic paeans to female anatomy, and then adding a couple of my own. I wrote in English, and in the count's hand, and signed it, "Your slave in love."

When Mrs. Quinlan arrived, she was taken at once to the study. It appeared the countess had planned a private tête-à-tête. The count was crestfallen—and my plan complicated. I would need to work through an agent.

I found Geneviève in the pantry preparing a tray of coffee and cakes. But for once, words escaped me. I thought it unlikely she would perform the errands I intended to assign her willingly. But neither could I think of anything with which to blackmail her. As luck would have it, she came to my aid.

"I believe someone was in my room the other evening...." She said it while smiling, but there was something serious behind it. "I don't know what you may have seen...."

She was fearful of something, something I might expose. But I was sure I had searched her room thoroughly and seen nothing that warranted such worry. The only things that stood out from the ordinary were the curious forms for darning socks.

"Do you need to darn many socks in that peculiar shape?"

"Darn socks?"

"Yes, those wooden forms. They were worn so incredibly smooth."

She laughed a little laugh—so very soft, and so *very* awkward. I had just what I needed. I wasn't sure what it was exactly, but all that really mattered was that *she* knew.

"I apologize for the invasion of your privacy," I said in my most solemn voice. "It was unspeakable. And if you will but forgive me, you may rest assured that *whatever* I saw is now forgotten."

By then, I'd had years of practice giving little speeches such as this, so the words came all too easily. And, just as I knew they would, they had the desired effect. She pulled me to her and kissed my face.

"You are a good little girl, aren't you?"

I don't know if she genuinely believed that. But if she did, there's little doubt my next utterance set her straight.

"I wondered if I might ask you a favor. Do you think you could slip this letter in Mrs. Quinlan's handbag?"

"Slip it into her handbag?"

"Yes, without the countess noticing. It's all right if Mrs. Quinlan sees you doing it, as I'm sure curiosity will prevent her from interfering. She carries quite a large handbag, so I don't think there will be much of a problem."

She looked at the envelope. "Isn't this the handwriting of the count?"

"You needn't worry about that."

"It's only, he gave me just such a note to give to the lady."

"May I see it?"

She reached in a pocket of her skirt and mechanically handed me a letter. I ripped it open. Not surprisingly, the count's English prose was even duller than his French. I tore it into small pieces.

"You may trust that mine is vastly superior. Say nothing to the count, of course. But give him this letter after you leave Mrs. Quinlan." It was a copy of Gwenie's second letter. "Tell him she slipped it to you without the countess being aware.... Now you had best be going. The coffee will be getting cold."

"Yes, of course."

I followed her up and then watched as she took the tray into the study. When she emerged, she gave me a guilty little nod and hurried off.

My task was completed. But being congenitally nosy, I couldn't help wondering why the countess would want to meet privately with this woman she seemed to barely know. The door was closed, but both women were clear speakers and my hearing has always been remarkably acute.

"How do you find it here in Washington?" the countess asked her.

"Well, I'd prefer New York, or even Boston. But... Have you ever been to Augusta?"

"No. I've not had the pleasure."

"You'd need a good deal more brandy in your coffee to think it that. It's at one remove from a logging camp. My husband has it in his head to return there and run for the governorship. Thankfully, I think I've convinced him to stay here, in the Senate."

"Did you know that he has been offered an ambassadorship?"

"No, he hasn't mentioned it. To where?"

"That's not definite. But Europe, certainly."

"Sounds terribly vague. I'm sure I can convince him to turn that down as well."

"I'm sure you could. But there are those who would be in your debt, if he were to choose to take the ambassadorship."

"Who exactly?"

"I will cut to the chase. Your husband chairs an important committee, a committee with legislation before it which some very well placed men hope to scuttle. Your husband is disinclined to do so. On the other hand, Senator Rogers, next in seniority, is in agreement with these well-placed men."

"So there is a conspiracy to get my husband out of Washington?"

"Put simply, yes. It was agents of this conspiracy who suggested that he could easily win the governorship. But I stepped in and put a stop to such talk."

"Then I should thank you."

"I told them they must think of the senator's young wife, exiled to that backwater. It was unthinkable. Have you been to Paris? Or London?"

"London only briefly, when I was just out of school. *Mais j'ai vécu à Paris pendant deux ans.*"

"*Madame, votre accent est superbe,*" the countess lied. Her accent was certainly not superb. "Of course, even if you weren't stationed in one of those cities, travel there is so easy, and so inexpensive."

"You want me to convince my husband to take this ambassadorship?"

"It does seem the most agreeable solution for everyone involved, don't you think?"

"Well, what I think is, if that's what these well-placed men desire of me, I should get something for my trouble. Some insurance, in case all I've done is exchange an American backwater for a European one."

"That is just what I told them."

"How much?"

"Ten thousand dollars in a New York bank under your name and your name alone."

"Twenty."

"I am authorized to go only as high as fifteen."

"All right, seventeen five."

"Done."

From there, the conversation drifted to the usual Washington gossip. Which, if you haven't been privy to it, consists mainly of exchanging anecdotes that put any not in attendance in the worst possible light. Poor Senator Quinlan bore the brunt of it.

Because my father was in the same line as the countess, I'd been eavesdropping on such dialogues since I was old enough to crawl. I loved and admired my father dearly, but in all honesty, he fell short of the subtle efficiency of the countess.

I moved from the door just as the captain came up the stairs. I saw he had picked up the letter awaiting him on the tray in the hall—my letter, of course. From his smile, I could tell he knew what I'd been up to. He wagged a finger at me in silent chastisement.

"*Fraternité,*" I whispered, defiantly.

His expression changed. Yes, he thought, she *does* know *something* about *something*.

I thanked him on behalf of Mrs. Bradley for the franc which was quickly forthcoming.

Just as he went off, the door to the study opened and I hurried downstairs.

"I'm so glad we were able to arrive at an amicable solution," the countess told her guest, as she escorted her down to the front hall. "And I'm sure you will come to enjoy the change."

"Oh, I will. ...One change or another."

Thomas was already holding Mrs. Quinlan's fur coat for her. It was an oversized thing and she needed to flop it onto her shoulders before buttoning it. When she'd gone, and Thomas had closed the door, I noticed a small book lying on the floor. I leaned down and picked it up. It had a beige cover, and an unfamiliar title.

"What's that?" the countess asked, her hand extended peremptorily.

"A book," I said while handing it to her. "I think it must have fallen when Mrs. Quinlan put on her coat. Shall I run after her?"

"Yes..." She was examining the cover. "No... No, wait." By now, she'd opened the book and was reading. "There's no need.... I'll give it to her later."

She walked upstairs with her eyes glued to Mrs. Quinlan's little volume.

I looked over at Thomas. He gave a small shrug.

After going to my room, I made up another envelope of phony correspondence for Mrs. Reese's husband, using the second letters of Gwenie and the captain. I can't say they meshed perfectly. The captain, though both eloquent and precise in his praise of a lady's form, was something of a traditionalist. Gwenie wrote lewd, and ran at only one speed: unbridled.

That evening the countess went out, so I took it upon myself to eat with the other guests in the dining room. I wanted to see if the letter from Captain Dumont had taken effect on Mrs. Reese. It had, but not in the way I had hoped. Instead of flirting with him, as she had most nights before, she stared at him whenever he was looking away from her, and became blushingly nervous when he wasn't. What's more, she seemed to have forgotten her French entirely.

With dessert, the subject of electrocution came up. Or rather, I brought it up, in the context of Chester Gillette's death sentence. I took some pride in my knowledge of both topics, so I was doubly put out when the others began explaining things to me. To begin with, Mrs. Reese suddenly became talkative. She had covered the trial for some English newspaper and was perhaps justified in thinking she was better acquainted with the facts of the case. Still, she wasn't nearly so good at filling in the unexplained details as Jessie and myself. She tried alluding to the victim's pregnancy in euphemisms she thought outside my understanding. She was wrong, of course. And it was I who had to set the count straight with a German term Miss Ditka had taught me.

As much as I loathed being lectured to by this would-be novelist (and, I might add, lackadaisical lover), the patronizing attitude of the two men was worse by far. They told me my figures for the electric power required to kill a man were all wrong. "Far too low," the captain said, then droned on about how amps multiplied by volts equals watts, and then divided by ohms equals something else. Or maybe it was the reverse. And the contemptible count was even ruder.

"It is *utterly impossible* to be electrocuted with less than *extraordinary* means," he said.

"That's not true. Just last week, a horse was electrocuted by a trolley wire up in Boston."

"A horse is not a man!"

"I don't see what difference it makes. And there was a man killed in a theatre while working on the lights...."

"Pish," he said—or at least the German equivalent.

The next morning, I took a street car downtown to Mr. Serby's emporium. Mr. Serby ran a secondhand clothing store, and I'd gone there once with Jessie when a guest of my parents had neglected to take home a cashmere scarf. I'm not certain what material the count's overcoat was made of, but it brought in $12 (less car fare and an ice cream soda) for the fund.

On returning to the house, I considered sending another of Gwenie's letters written in Mrs. Reese's hand to the captain, but decided she was simply not the type of woman who would take the plunge. However, that didn't mean my efforts at sparking a jealous rage in her husband wouldn't bear fruit. I prepared yet another envelope, with a copy of Gwenie's incomparable final letter. I even managed to reproduce its sticky feel.

5

That afternoon, I noticed Thomas outside polishing the auto. Even for a servant as attentive as he was, this struck me as taking things too far. It was bitterly cold, and he wasn't even wearing a hat. I found a nice thick one and brought it out to him. He took the hat, and smiled at me weakly. I could see at once that he'd been crying. Though I was shivering fearfully, I refused to leave until he told me the cause of his sorrow. Finally, after I'd taken back the thick hat and placed it on myself, he assented.

"This morning, I saw Captain Dumont come out of the countess's bedchamber."

"Is that all? Do you mean you only just noticed that he's been visiting her at night?" I asked.

"The visits are bad enough. But *him* she allows to stay until morning! Not even the first count was allowed that."

I found that curious, but it seemed hardly the time to press him for details. "Well, I am working on the problem. You'll have to trust me, Thomas. And have some patience."

"But I'm afraid there is so little time. The countess is planning a party for New Year's Eve. A very large affair. I fear it is then she will announce her betrothal."

His news surprised me, as I'd assumed that the countess had sworn off marriage. But I maintained my confident manner for the sake of my friend. "Not if I can help it. I've opened several lines of attack, but the more the better. We must think. Is there any stone we've left unturned?"

He shook his head gloomily. I could see it would all be up to me. Fortunately, I am rarely at a loss for new ways to make mischief.

"Didn't I see a gift from the captain for the countess under the tree?" I asked. "And one from her to him, as well?"

"Yes. They both seemed very pleased with what they had found."

"Were they? Well, then I suspect there will be some surprises come Christmas."

"What do you mean?"

"It's simple! We'll replace their gifts with ones less likely to please—far less likely."

While the countess and her guests were having dinner, Thomas and I went out shopping. All the stores were open late that week and the lavish displays of toys, candies, and sundry other enticements made it difficult for me to remain focused on our mission. Not so Thomas.

He took me to the least opulent of the department stores, the sort of place neither the countess nor the captain would be likely to set foot in. For Dumont's gift to the countess, he chose a set of ready-made monogrammed handkerchiefs—in cotton! I commended his choice most heartily.

The countess's gift to the captain was obviously a small book, of similar dimensions to the one dropped by Mrs. Quinlan the afternoon before. It was quite simple finding a replacement of the appropriate size and tediousness. There was a whole shelf of humdrum octavos in the store's book department. We chose one on raising homing pigeons.

Late that night, Thomas came to my door and tapped gently. I was waiting. In our stocking feet, we crept downstairs and into the parlor, where the tree had been set up. It wasn't anything as impressive as ours at home, but there were some painted ornaments which rewarded inspection. They were peopled with couples wearing archaic fashions (at least, for the most part still wearing them) and indulging various fancies amidst delightfully Edenic gardens. And they all seemed to be having a *very* good time.

For two old hands like us, the substitution of the gifts was the work of a moment. Our book was nearly identical in size to the one it replaced. And the captain had set his equally modest-sized gift in a large box, perhaps to puzzle the countess before the unwrapping. The handkerchiefs fit perfectly. Once the replacement gifts were packaged and placed under the tree, Thomas proposed to destroy the others lest they be discovered.

"No—I may have use for them. You do still wish me to get rid of the count, don't you?"

"Yes... but if the countess should see you with the book she meant for the captain..."

He didn't need to finish his sentence. I was well aware that there were distinct limits to the countess's indulgence which even I would be wise not to test.

"You needn't worry. Both will be out of my hands tomorrow."

I took the two gifts with me up to my room. As I crept by the bedroom of the count, I heard voices, then noticed a band of light below the door. Once I'd deposited the presents in my room, I went back to see what was going on. Herr Kirsch was helping his master dress. The count was a handsome man, and looked particularly so now. He placed a hothouse carnation in his lapel while carefully surveying himself in the mirror.

"*Voilà!*"

I thought for a moment he might be planning a visit to Mrs. Quinlan, but several references were then made to "*die Fräulein.*"

They seemed to be preparing to leave, so I started to move away from the keyhole. Then I realized that they were going through the door to the servants' hall. I hurried down the front stairs and tiptoed into the darkened kitchen. Herr Kirsch led the count down the back stairs to the little entryway off the kitchen and there provided his master with a top hat and a substitute overcoat. The valet now opened the door and said something in German. I believe he was telling the count a cab was waiting around the corner. He handed him a key and then the count left.

Herr Kirsch closed the door, but instead of going upstairs he simply stood there and waited. It seemed like an hour, but may have just been a few minutes. Then he put on his own overcoat and hat, which he kept on the stand by the door (cashmere and sable, I noted—Mr. Serby would be most impressed).

It was only when he'd gone that I dared to breathe— and likewise Geneviève. She was seated just a few feet from where I was standing. I assume she was as ignorant of my presence as I was of hers because she gave a little yelp.

"I woke feeling very hungry," I told her.

"Yes, I too."

She turned on the light and warmed some milk, then put out some pie left over from dinner. I think she would have been happy to forget what we'd seen, but not me.

"I presume the count has a lady friend."

"From what Herr Kirsch tells me, he has many."

"And him, too, apparently."

"Perhaps."

She seemed contemplative. I noticed then that her eyes were red, as if she'd been crying. I'd touched on a sensitive subject.

We ate quietly for some time, until we heard a key in the lock. Geneviève quickly turned off the light. It was Gustave, no doubt returning from a late evening at Gwenie's. He turned the light back on and seemed to take our presence in stride. He dispatched an inebriated smile, then in French told Geneviève that she'd better get to bed as they would need to rise early for the baking.

I'm not sure what time I got back to my room. I was quite tired, but curiosity overruled fatigue and so I immediately set to examining the gifts we'd removed from under the tree.

The one from the captain was in a small box which had been taped to the bottom of the larger one which now held the monogrammed handkerchiefs. Inside was a vial of perfume. It bore the *name Deux nuits d'excès*. The bottle was sealed with a ribbon affixed in such a way that any intrusion would be obvious. Its provocative appellation, however, proved an irresistible lure. I couldn't be sure what was meant by "two nights of excess," but I knew it must be good. I tore away the seal.

The scent operated on me in the strangest way imaginable. Within seconds, I felt compelled to run my fingers through my hair, then to caress my cheek. In my carelessness, I spilt some on the countess's gift to the captain. This accident delivered me from my delirium. I returned to the work I had before me. I used a length of hair ribbon to resecure the stopper to the bottle, and then returned it to the box.

The now-scented book bore the title *Gamiani*, and, I assumed not coincidentally, the subtitle *Deux nuits d'excès*. It had a beige cover, just like the one dropped by Mrs. Quinlan. I believe I even detected a dent where it had hit the tile floor of the hall. It was in French, and the more telling details were related mostly through poetic euphemism. Without a dictionary, I couldn't make much headway. But from what I was able to glean, I knew it to be a *very* naughty book—and one I should be reluctant to part with. I made plans to recover it once I'd put it to use.

The next day, a Wednesday, after a diversion of some hours brought on by my sampling of the perfume and consequent revelry (about which the less said the better), I rewrapped and readdressed the gifts.

The book had borne an inscription from the countess hinting that if the captain presented her with a certain proposal, he would not be disappointed. So Thomas's fears were not misplaced. I'd had to carefully cut out this fly-leaf. On its reverse was an engraved frontispiece which conveyed the thrust of the book quite nakedly (I still have it, if you are interested). I wrote a new, simpler inscription: *In anticipation*. With the book, I included the already prepared copy of Gwenie's third, most lurid letter—the one addressed to "Sword of my sheath," and signed with the damp lips colored in blood.

The perfume was repackaged with a letter from the count to Mrs. Quinlan. He told her how she had driven him to distraction and that he must see her soon or expire. He remembered her husband mentioning that he'd be traveling through the middle of the week (which he had), and suggested she visit his chamber that night.

The rear door of the house would be unlocked, and he drew a map explaining how to approach his room from the servants' hall.

Fearing Thomas might feel I was overreaching, I refrained from informing him about the invitation. I frankly saw little hope that the lady would be so venturesome as to take such a chance, but gambled on the likelihood that a servant would read the note and share its contents with the senator, thus exposing her imaginary tryst with the count.

Thomas sent Geneviève to deliver the gift to Mrs. Quinlan, with strict orders to hand it to her in person. This was an idea of mine, as I figured it would make whichever servant who waited on Geneviève mad with curiosity. When told the lady was out of town for the day, the maid obediently brought the gift back. No matter, I thought. Tomorrow will do just as well.

That same afternoon, a wire arrived for Mrs. Reese. As the messenger waited for a reply, I took it up to her room. Naturally, I read it on the way. It was from her husband, asking if he should join her in Washington. He made no mention of the letters I'd been sending him, but clearly they'd had an effect—just not as much of an effect as I'd hoped.

Since lurid letters had failed to stir the do-nothing to action, I thought I would try another tack: brevity. While Mrs. Reese made out her reply to the wire, I went to my room and prepared a letter of a single line for the same correspondent: "The writing of love notes is over...."

When the others had gathered in the dining room that night, I placed the wrapped gift for the count on his pillow. I would leave him to wonder how it had been delivered, as it could only deepen the mystery of the romance he so obviously found to his liking.

During my visit to his room, I made economical use of my time and examined it thoroughly. One never knows what one may find. I turned on the lamp which sat next to a pitcher of water on a little table beside the bed. The lamp flickered some, and I noticed a leg of the table was pinching the cord. I freed it, but could see the cord had become frayed. I considered bringing this to someone's attention, but decided not to risk having my caution ridiculed as illogical.

There was a noise in the servants' hall and I quickly made my way through the main door.

6

I spent Thursday morning composing a second letter from the captain's fiancée. As you may have already guessed, her resistance to the charms of the rich and handsome suitor was weakening. Her every inch yet yearned for masculine attention, and her being still begged for the completion which only a man can provide a woman. But somehow that didn't seem enough. Since I'd never utilized Gwenie's ultimate letter for the faux correspondence from Mrs. Reese (only in the reconstruction of that faux correspondence created for the benefit of her husband, as I'm sure you remember), I decided to use French translations of some of her more lickerish phraseology.

Fashioning a convincing envelope proved more problematic than the letter itself. I'd hoped to make use of the one the first letter arrived in. The captain had left for the embassy, so I made a thorough search of his room. I could find no trace of that letter, or the one I'd sent over the name of Mrs. Reese. I assumed he must have destroyed them lest the countess or servants catch sight of them. I suppose it was for that same reason he kept no photographs of the girl in Paris.

I remembered I'd seen some letters from France in Geneviève's room and asked her if I could have the stamps for my collection. Naturally, she agreed. Anything, I imagine, to prevent another of my visits to her room. I detached the stamps and pasted them to my new envelope, even recreating cancellation marks. I only wish

Miss Ditka had been there to see the results.

The captain returned for lunch and took the letter to his room. A little later, during the meal, I could tell from his face he was mulling his options. Whenever the countess looked away, he surveyed her intently—no doubt comparing her to his memory of that oh-so-plain girl back in France. We could only hope that her fortune trumped his memory.

From the moment Thomas enlisted my help, I had tried to create whatever friction I could between the count and captain. This wasn't terribly difficult. Though he had won the countess's affections, the captain was jealous of the count, perhaps fearing the finicky woman would go back to him. For the count, I think, it was more a matter of pride than jealousy. He thought the captain his social inferior and couldn't abide being replaced by him, even if he too had tired of his affair with the countess. But what he resented most about the Frenchman was his quick wit and the playful barbs which not infrequently were aimed at himself.

That afternoon, both the count and the countess went off to some function at the German Embassy. Then, almost immediately after their departure, Herr Kirsch went off, acting—as the newspapers would say—quite furtively.

When next Mrs. Reese left the house, saying she'd be shopping until dinner, I suggested to Thomas he dispatch Geneviève back to Mrs. Quinlan's to make her delivery. I saw an opportunity shaping up and wasn't certain of the maid's allegiance.

The way now clear, I approached the captain.

"This is our chance!" I told him.

"Our chance?"

"To get even with that dreadful count! You can't deny he's insufferable."

"No, I don't deny that. What is it you have in mind?"

"To soak him in bed!"

"Soak him?"

I took the captain upstairs and showed him the pitcher of water on the table beside the bed.

"But what will you do, come in and pour it over him?"

"Nothing so foolish as that. What we need is some way to topple the pitcher while both of us are safely out of the room. I thought you... being a captain of engineers..."

He smiled and made a little nod.

I sometimes wonder whether, if you made it a matter of ego, a man couldn't be convinced to contrive his own execution. (Oh, don't worry, my dear, just some idle musing.)

"Ah. I have an idea," he said, after considering carefully the room and its furnishings. "However, someone will need to set it in motion."

"Set it in motion how?"

"Well, say by opening a door."

"Geneviève brings the count his breakfast every morning."

"And he eats it in bed?"

"Yes.... Sometimes with her sitting beside him."

"Little spy!" he teased. "That would work.... I only would hate to have him blame the girl."

"But won't it be obvious she wasn't behind it?"

"Yes, I suppose.... All right, what we need is a... *poulie?*"

"*Poulie?*"

He pantomimed pulling a rope to raise something.

"A pulley.... Come!"

I took him into the servants' hall and showed him the dumbwaiter.

"*Ah, parfait!*"

He immediately set to work, sending me to fetch various tools and materials from the carriage house: screwdrivers, pliers, cord, and a saw, among other things. It took hours and he was still finishing when Thomas alerted us that the countess had telephoned for him to pick her up in the auto.

We'd just given his device a dry run—both figuratively and literally—when we heard the front door close. Quickly, we moved everything into place. I peeked out the door and saw the countess coming upstairs. We crept out into the servants' hall and then down the rear stairs.

But the trap still needed to be set. Then, as the captain pointed out, we would need to make sure no one used the servants' door before the count was in bed. And that wouldn't be until after his valet attended him that evening. While we discussed this, I could sense that Captain Dumont was having second thoughts. Perhaps he was contemplating the count's dueling scar.

"Don't worry," I told him. "I know what needs to be done."

He patted my head and handed me a contribution for the fund. Another franc. I looked at it without enthusiasm, then slowly raised my eyes to his—a little performance well worth the silver dollar that followed.

I passed through the kitchen, into the dining room. Geneviève was there, setting the table.

"Did Mrs. Quinlan accept delivery of her gift?" I asked.

"She did. But she was very nervous. She had me shown up to her sitting room. While I waited, she read the letter and then opened the gift. She liked the perfume. Very much. Then she wrote a little note."

She handed me a folded piece of paper. The note consisted of three brief words: *I will come!*

It was madness. A senator's wife visiting the home of another woman for an assignation with one of her guests? That intoxicating perfume—it had left her without inhibition. Oh, why had I ever let it out of my hands!

This, however, was not my only regret. I now realized the very complexity of my plans might prove their greatest weakness. I'd sown so many seeds of deceit, even I had trouble determining which shoots constituted my intended garden and which were mere weeds. My mood darkened.

Then, about seven that evening, I glimpsed a ray of sunlight—metaphoric sunlight, as the sun had long since set, but welcome just the same. Harry Reese had arrived.

As with his wife, I'd met him before also and recognized him as soon as Thomas opened the door. He didn't seem as agitated as I'd hoped. And from the cool way the countess greeted him, I feared she would turn him out. She took him up to her study and I dutifully positioned myself at the keyhole.

My messages to him had worked with effect. But my efforts were to some extent undermined (and my well-being quite possibly imperiled) when the fool showed his hostess one of the letters Captain Dumont had supposedly written his wife.

Luckily, she laughed, and I could once more breathe. "I think I can guess who sent you this."

My feelings on hearing this were mixed. My keen

survival instinct led me to *hope* she suspected someone else. But my all-consuming ego was not so lily-livered.

She showed him the original I'd returned to her desk, the one addressed to her. He didn't seem to know what to make of this. Of course, he was one of those people of whom you can never be sure. Is he a master of inscrutability, or merely an imbecile? Such a fine line.

Thomas came upstairs carrying the new guest's suitcase. I watched until he'd gone back down, then slipped into the room Mr. Reese would be sharing with his wife. I'd barely had time to open the bag when he came in himself.

"I thought I'd help you unpack."

He eyed me warily.

"We met before," I said. "Don't you remember?"

"Yes, I remember. How's life in the land of the Great and Powerful Oz?"

"Oh, I outgrew that long ago. I read novels now."

"Well, just don't take up the writing of them. It enfeebles the mind."

"I will make every effort to heed your valuable advice."

Now he was really wary.

"Do you have any spare change?" I asked.

"Why, are you on the bum?"

"My bum?"

He smiled and tossed me a dime.

"It's for Mrs. Bradley's defense fund."

"Sounds suspiciously noble."

"It *is* noble!"

"Then I regret having been hoodwinked into contributing."

This annoyed me.

"Not so much as you'll regret losing your wife's affections."

"What would you know about my wife's affections?"

"Quite a lot. I could be of great help to you. If you're wise, you'll reassess your attitude toward the fund." I held out a hand and he gave me another dime. I stared at it until he added a quarter.

Just then, Mrs. Reese entered the room. She looked at her husband, then at me, then back at her husband.

"What in the world are you doing here, Harry?"

"I suppose you two have much to discuss," I said. Before departing, I gave them a little curtsey. Now they both looked at me warily.

I listened to what followed, of course, but it didn't amount to much. After his meeting with the countess, he felt unsure of his ground. He voiced some vague suspicions, and she deflected them with various noises. She had quite a repertoire of noises. Some fully formed syllables, some little more than exhalations, but all seeming to blend skepticism with derision.

He asked how her biography of the countess was progressing, and she told him well.

"It may not be the book I intended, but I'm certain that this time *something* will come of it."

"Is the lady cooperating?"

"Cooperating may not be the right word. But she is, in her way, contributing."

"I see. Is she aware she's contributing?"

He'd echoed my thought. She responded with a new noise. The font was bottomless.

At dinner, they both appeared uncomfortable, but she more so than him. The countess demonstrated her displeasure at his arrival by remaining aloof, while the captain busily sized the newcomer up. By dessert, he'd apparently decided the man posed no threat and had taken to teasing him.

Meanwhile, the count seemed lost in a world of his own—no doubt enraptured by the image of Mrs. Quinlan's *insatiable, gaping maw of passion*....

He went up right after dinner and took his customary bath. When I heard him tell Herr Kirsch he could retire, I knew my way was clear and crept into the empty bedchamber. Setting the trap simply involved tying two ends of cord to little hooks already in place, one on the servants' door, and the other attached to a block of wood keeping the table level.

The chanciest part of the operation came now. Since I couldn't depart as I had entered, via the servants' hall, I ran the risk of being seen leaving the room. I opened the door without a sound—my precaution of having the doors oiled now yielding a valuable dividend. I saw no one about, but noticed the door to the Reeses' room was slightly ajar. As I closed my own door, I heard another close just as softly.

7

As soon as I felt sure everyone had gone to their rooms for the night, I crept down to the kitchen and unlocked the back door. Then I turned on the kitchen light in case Mrs. Quinlan had trouble finding her way in the unfamiliar surroundings. No sooner had I done so than I heard someone coming down the servants' stairs from the third floor. I turned out the light and hid beneath the kitchen table. It was Gustave. He took his hat and coat from the stand, then came to the table. I feared he may have seen me in the dim light, but he was only picking up a box of pastries. Now he went out and locked the door.

I once more unlocked it. But then, just as before, I heard someone coming down from the third floor. Out went the light, and back under the table went I. This time it was Herr Kirsch. He too took a hat and coat from the stand and went out, locking the door behind him.

For the third time, I unlocked the door and turned on the light. I had just turned to leave when I heard someone outside. So it was back again under the table.

It was the lady herself. She was wrapped up in her huge coat and her head topped with a fur hat. She'd shivered when she entered, but then seemed nearly overcome by the heat. The coat dropped to the floor and the hat followed. She shivered again, but evidently not from the cold. Her eyes had an uncommon intensity, and rather than the intricate knot exhibited previously, her hair hung loosely about her flushed face. If I had to choose just one word to describe her, it would be sultry.

So simple a word, and yet one holding so much promise.

Somewhat undermining the effect was the heavy gown she wore, clearly selected for warmth rather than fashion. (This infelicity was not lost on her, however, as would soon become apparent.) She held the map I'd drawn in her hand. She studied it. Once oriented, she hurried up the back stairs to the second-floor servants' hall. While she did that, I scooted up the front stairs and positioned myself at the door connecting the main hall with the servants'. There was a dim light always on there and my view via the keyhole unimpeded. I saw her just outside the count's door. She checked her map again to make sure it was the correct door, then let the gown fall to her feet. Beneath it, she wore a negligee of the sheerest silk imaginable. Any sheerer and it would have ceased to exist altogether.

She took a deep breath, then opened the door. Just as I'd hoped, there was an exclamation from the count. He, and his bed, had been soaked.

Looking back, I feel fairly certain I hadn't anticipated what followed—or, at least, not consciously. But who can say with any assurance what her subliminal self is up to? Had she, without ever mentioning it, connected the frayed cord with the pitcher of water? Certainly a fascinating notion, and one I hope you'll find worthy of contemplation.

Whether by accident or unconscious design, the lights did indeed go out. I could now hear Mrs. Quinlan fumbling in the darkness. But just as I was about to go to her aid, someone entered the hall mere feet from where I was positioned.

"Is someone there?" she whispered. It was Mrs. Reese.

I said nothing, then listened as she felt her way to the bathroom.

Next, Mrs. Quinlan came out from the servants' hall, apparently lost.

"I can help you downstairs," I whispered.

"I... Yes...." She spoke like a somnambulist.

I was just reaching for her hand when I sensed someone emerging from the room Mrs. Reese had just left. He walked clumsily toward the stairs, then called down in a low voice, "Anyone there?" It was Mr. Reese, of course. Meanwhile, his wife emerged from the bathroom and passed within inches of myself and Mrs. Quinlan. I think she must have heard her husband, but rather than reply, she tiptoed into their room. I reached once more for Mrs. Quinlan's hand, hoping to lead her back into the servants' hall and down the back stairs. But she was gone.

I began frantically feeling about the dark hall. Then I heard her startled intake of breath, followed by a queer sort of groan. She'd connected with Mr. Reese at the far end of the hall.

"Is that you, Emmie?" he asked.

"Yes.... Yes, darling, it's me," she told him. "Go on back to bed and I'll be with you shortly."

Then I heard her kiss him! And it wasn't some perfunctory peck. I believe he was similarly impressed by her enthusiasm, because he proceeded to do just as he was told.

I thought this very clever of the lady, clearing the way for her escape. But I was wrong. Once she'd ascertained which room he retreated to, she followed, just as she had promised. It was quite mad.

With her on the very threshold of the room, I acted.

To this day, I regret not having taken the time to more carefully weigh the possibilities. Who knows in what interesting way Mrs. Reese might have reacted on the lady joining the conjugal bed?

At the time, however, I was thinking only of how the *countess* would react were *she* awakened. Quite possibly, she would be amused. Nonetheless, I decided that no matter how short the odds, this was a wager I could not afford to make.

I grabbed Mrs. Quinlan roughly by the arm. "It's a trap," I whispered.

"A trap…," she replied.

"Come, quickly, or we'll wake the countess. And we mustn't annoy her. Remember the bank account in New York."

"Yes…. Seventeen five…."

Apparently, there were quantifiable limits to her irrationality.

I led her down the front stairs and into the kitchen. Just as we entered, the lights came back on. Geneviève was revealed seated at the table and looking again as if she'd been crying. She was naturally surprised to see us, but too distracted to speak.

"You'd better go up to bed," I said. "And it would be best to forget about this."

She nodded, then slowly climbed the back stairs.

I picked up Mrs. Quinlan's coat for her.

"My gown…," she said.

I ran up the back stairs. I found Geneviève in the second-floor servants' hall. She was looking into the count's room through the still-open door. It was dark, as his lamp had not come back on.

"You must go to bed!" I told her.

I closed the door and picked up the gown, then led her to the stairs. Once she ascended, I went back down to Mrs. Quinlan. Thomas had just come up from the basement, where he'd been replacing the fuse. He and Mrs. Quinlan now stood staring at each other with equal interest.

I handed her the gown. As she stepped into it, I addressed the stupefied butler.

"I've no time to explain now, but we must help Mrs. Quinlan to get home as quickly as possible. Can you take her in the auto?"

"Yes, of course." He helped her on with her coat and hat, then took her out to the auto.

No sooner had they driven off than Herr Kirsch arrived. He looked different, not so cool as usual. He became nervous on seeing me, offering some silly explanation of having gone out for some air. He hung up his hat and coat, and then as he went up the back stairs, I went up the front ones to my room.

I slept surprisingly well the remainder of the night. All I knew with certainty at that point was that the count's lamp had burned out. Who was I to dare suspect the nobleman had been wrong in his calculations concerning the lethal potential of household current?

I had breakfast in the kitchen. Kirsch was at the table with a now-chipper Geneviève and I assumed it was his presence which had brought on her change of mood. There's no accounting for taste. They and Gustave all conversed in French, and rather than spend the meal translating, I scoured the newspaper for stories with which I could regale Jessie on her return. I did not need to scour far. Somehow I had missed a case every bit as sordid as that of Mrs. Bradley.

It seems that six days before, two brothers in Culpepper, Virginia, had killed a man named Bywaters. The Strothers, as the brothers were named, had earlier that day encouraged Bywaters to come to their home and marry their sister, and he had complied. Once the ceremony was completed, however, Bywaters attempted to leave the house. So the brothers shot him.

An odd scenario, and it took some research into the prior days' newspapers to sort things out. Apparently, Bywaters had seduced the sister, and when it became obvious she was carrying a child, he took her into Washington for an "illegal operation." This was a favorite circumlocution of the newspapers which Jessie had explained to me a month before—and in the most gruesome terms imaginable. Jessie could make a trip to the zoo seem decadent—"Oh, look how that Johnny-no-good lion's tryin' ta get his hooks on 'er here-after. Leave 'er alone, ya devil!"—so you can imagine her rendition of a trip to an abortionist.

The sister was still recovering in bed from some after-effect of the botched operation when her husband of an hour tried to abandon her and her brothers dispatched him. Now charged with murder, the Strothers had become a worthy cause. I went and created a little box for their fund. The timing was fortunate because I'd by then hit up everyone in the household several times over on behalf of Mrs. Bradley. Geneviève contributed a dime, and Herr Kirsch did likewise. Thomas gave me a whole pocketful of change, but Gustave was merely sympathetic.

I then went into the dining room to torment the guests. The Reeses were there with Captain Dumont. I particularly enjoyed outmaneuvering Mr. Reese, for not only was he onto me, he made no attempt to hide his disapproval of the subtle blackmail I practiced. In the course of that morning, he contributed a further $1.25 to Mrs. Bradley's fund, and then two bits for the Strothers. And I, in turn, was able to furnish information leading to the recovery of his overcoat.

Of course, a good deal else went on that morning. The countess came down about half past nine and, as was her custom at the breakfast table, ignored her guests. Then, maybe ten minutes later, Thomas entered the room and informed her that the count had been electrocuted.

I don't think I'm boasting when I say no one exhibited more surprise than myself—a bravura performance that went unseen and unappreciated. Captain Dumont's surprise, on the other hand, was both more genuine and more closely observed. I feared, briefly, that he would give things away by confessing his part in the affair. But he would soon enough make evident the extent of his cowardice.

Thomas was sent for a doctor, and Mr. Reese was directed to look into the matter upstairs. I snuck out after him and at once took up position just outside the count's open door.

Inside the count's room, Herr Kirsch showed Mr. Reese the frayed cord, and then the captain's contraption. I'd not given the valet credit for being so clever. Mr. Reese seemed more apprehensive than intrigued. The countess had made clear her wish that the affair be handled as quietly as possible.

It was about then that Captain Dumont passed me going to his room at the end of the hall. There was no *Fraternité* this time. I don't think he even noticed me.

A moment later, Thomas and the doctor came up the stairs and entered the dead man's chamber. After examining the corpse, the doctor pronounced cardiac arrest as the cause of death. But he was disinclined to believe it had been brought on by electrocution. It seemed so gallant, the way certain of these men were determined to exonerate my subliminal self. Even the count himself, if only posthumously.

Just as Herr Kirsch was giving the doctor a demonstration of the contraption behind the bureau, Captain Dumont emerged from his room carrying two pieces of luggage. He tiptoed past the count's door, unobserved by all but me.

"*Fraternité,*" I whispered.

The captain looked back at me nervously, then set down the bags and reached in his pocket.

He handed me a ten-dollar gold piece and put a finger to his lips. I smiled and gave him a little curtsey. I don't think I reassured him, as he paused and looked at me now even more nervously than before. Finally, he picked up his bags and proceeded down the stairs with me just behind.

He had some trouble locating his hat and coat, but I was soon able to turn them up. There's something about a ten-dollar gold piece that makes an impression.

The countess came and embraced him, then pushed him out the door. I think his exit affected her. But on seeing me watching, her expression hardened. I couldn't be certain if she simply didn't want to be seen being emotive, or if she suspected the part I played in her lover's departure. Either way, I thought it advisable to fade into the background and did so posthaste.

The countess went back to the table and made some

innocuous comment about the weather to Mrs. Reese, the only one remaining. That lady replied hesitantly, as if she feared taking a position on whether we should expect snow or not might entail an unforeseeable risk.

8

Thomas, with Mr. Reese and Herr Kirsch in tow, reentered the dining room not five minutes after the captain's departure. They confirmed, one after another, that the count had been murdered. Their conclusion annoyed the countess—and their dogmatism me. To call it murder seemed the height of hyperbole. Nevertheless, I thought it an inopportune time to voice objections.

Apprehending the inevitability of police involvement, the countess instructed Mr. Reese to telephone a policeman, one whom he and his wife agreed was of a suitably pliable disposition. When he returned from his call, Mr. Reese asked the whereabouts of Captain Dumont. The countess announced that he had left for New York, and from there would be sailing for France. When it was suggested his exit invited suspicion, the lady became indignant, then offhandedly provided the Frenchman an alibi at the cost of her virtue, a currency she valued little.

The policeman who'd been called in was a Sergeant Lacy. He had investigated a jewelry theft at our home five years before, which wasn't really a jewelry theft at all. But that's another story.

He was not like other policemen, who by and large come in only one variety: dull. He was more like a fictional depiction of a policeman, if you can imagine. His language was affected, his gestures theatrical, and his bearing pompous. In all other ways, however, he was the typical cop, worried more about his pension and perquisites than bringing the guilty to justice. I, for one, was much relieved at the choice.

Mr. Reese took him up to the count's room and his wife and I jockeyed for position at the keyhole. The sergeant seemed inclined to ascribe guilt to Herr Kirsch, even though it was the valet himself who had uncovered the device by which the count had met his death.

Having seen all she wanted, Mrs. Reese went across the hall to her room. I saw her gaze back at me before closing her door. It was a quizzical look, and not the first she'd given me that morning.

Sometime later a police surgeon was brought to the count's room and I planted myself at the keyhole of the servants' hall door. He too was skeptical of electrocution as the cause of death, conjecturing that the surprise of being doused with water might have been enough to induce shock. What an accommodating man. His rather simple explanation hadn't even occurred to me.

No sooner had he left than the men from the morgue came to take away the body. When they removed the quilt still partially covering the count, the book he'd been reading fell to the floor. Mr. Reese picked it up. He sniffed it, then put it in his pocket. It was *Gamiani*, of course. I couldn't imagine what he wanted it for, but I was determined to get it back before he left town.

That afternoon, the sergeant began questioning suspects in the billiard room. The first was Geneviève. She imparted the news that the previous maid was let go for some indiscretion involving the count. Because of that, she said, she assiduously avoided any intimacy with him.

I suppose it comes down to what one considers intimacy. I'd seen her sitting on his bed and playfully positioning a napkin at his breast. While her hands were thus occupied, his right one was hidden from view, its disposition only given away when she emitted a sharp yelp and leapt off the bed.

She also denied having any interest in Herr Kirsch—a patent lie. They flirted constantly, and I'd seen her weeping at the kitchen door whenever he went off on his late-night visits to who knows what trollop.

When she was dismissed, the detective summoned the cook, and then Mrs. Reese to act as translator. I needed to quickly hide myself behind the Christmas tree when Mr. Reese left the room to fetch his wife, and then race back to the keyhole after their return. Household spying, done properly, is a contest requiring swift maneuver. But in this case, well worth the effort. For what happened next was not at all what I expected.

It looked like a sort of inquisition, with Gustave seated and the others all standing before him. The sergeant would pose some question, such as, "What are your feelings about Geneviève?" After Mrs. Reese translated it, the cook would reply in French with something innocuous like, "She's a nice girl, don't you think?"

But instead of reporting what he'd said, Mrs. Reese would offer some wild interpretation, such as, "He says, 'I can't stop thinking of her. I lie awake at night, my work suffers, I squander my money on her...,'" etc.

The sergeant asked if the cook suspected the count was having better luck with the maid. Mrs. Reese translated this as a query about what the count preferred for breakfast. When the cook told her that Geneviève brought him coffee and croissants late each morning, she asked how many croissants. "Sometimes two or three," the cook told her.

Her English translation of this dialogue was that

Geneviève visited the count at night. Sometimes two or three times in one night. When the cook said Geneviève was so partial to croissants herself that she risked getting fat, Mrs. Reese rendered this as, "She was so insatiable, she risked getting pregnant," deliberately choosing the figurative meaning of the word *grosse* over the literal one.

It seemed that Mrs. Reese wished to make it appear that the cook had killed the count out of jealousy over Geneviève. I could think of only one explanation for her behavior. She must have realized Captain Dumont was responsible for the device behind the bureau and was now trying to give him time to escape. Perhaps the letter she'd received from him (or me acting as him) had won her heart. I was almost as touched as I was flattered.

That evening, the countess went out and the Reeses ate alone in the dining room. I spied on them through the soup and salad, but they treated each other with such wariness, I learned nothing of use. I do hope, my dear, that we won't be similarly so suspicious of one another.

Taking Mrs. Reese's efforts on behalf of the captain as my cue, I spent the rest of the evening composing a letter in the Frenchman's elegant hand. It was directed to the count and warned him to cease directing his attentions toward a woman who remained nameless but was described as having "languid eyes, a button nose, and lubricious lips." I thought these three traits enough to point to Mrs. Reese. Particularly, the lubricious lips—she was forever rubbing balm on them.

I wasn't attempting to implicate her in the count's death, of course, merely trying to deflect suspicion from Gustave and Geneviève. It seemed to me she had taken things a little too far. Especially given the depths of the policeman's naiveté.

The next morning, Sergeant Lacy arrived promptly at half past eight looking for breakfast. I brought him into the dining room, then gave him the letter I told him I'd seen the count toss out. He was most interested.

When Mr. Reese came down, the detective pocketed the letter. Then, after some distractions about marmalade and the inoperative dumbwaiter, he began constructing a scenario whereby Mr. Reese killed the count out of jealousy over his wife. I hadn't intended my letter to trigger this line of reasoning, but wasn't surprised that it did. What did surprise me was how Mrs. Reese responded. When she came down, she immediately entered into the discussion and, without prompting, volunteered as evidence in support of the sergeant's theory a past episode in which her husband became violent toward a suspected suitor of hers. What was she up to, I wondered.

Her husband, it seems, was wondering the same thing. Once Sergeant Lacy had left the room, and I had disappeared from view—albeit without sacrificing my proximity—he asked her just that. She evaded the question, but, with what sounded curiously like coyness, told him she would like to try "that perfume." He reminded her he had given her a book instead. It didn't take me long to deduce he'd given her *my* book! *Gamiani*, I mean. She must have smelled the perfume I'd gotten on it and now wanted that as well. At the mention of a new negligee (her tone lending it connotations beyond those of mere underwear), I made my presence known.

I loved surprising adults, but few offered the fun Mrs. Reese did. The least I could do in return was assist her in wiping up her spilt coffee.

By then, Sergeant Lacy and Mr. Reese had gone to the billiard room to continue their consultations regarding the count's death. It was my plan to again listen in from the parlor, but as I passed through the hall, I saw the doctor's hat still on the table. Thomas had expressed his intention of driving downtown that morning and I thought I would catch a ride to Mr. Serby's store. I took the doctor's hat and coat out to the auto, but couldn't locate Thomas. I was on my way upstairs when Mr. Reese passed me on his way down. He asked me where Geneviève was and I told him she was in the kitchen doing dishes.

As I went toward my room, I saw Sergeant Lacy in Captain Dumont's room. I crept up and could see he was looking through a stack of letters. He had found a secret compartment in the captain's trunk!

I won't deny the self-recrimination I felt at not having noticed it in my own search. Then I saw the money. A good deal of money. Four thick stacks of twenty-dollar bills. What I felt now went well beyond self-recrimination.

The precise sequence of events which followed has become clouded with time. But I think it ran nearly like this. The stacks of currency called to me like a siren. I doubt it comes as a revelation that there's a not insubstantial streak of venality which runs through me. I come by it honestly, inherited from my father. But that was only the half of it. I now had *two* worthy causes of wronged womanhood for which to procure funds. Poor Mrs. Bywaters, still recovering in bed, her brothers, quite absurdly, charged with murder. She needed my help desperately. As did Mrs. Bradley. The newspapers were now busily sullying her name, gratuitously pointing out that she bore the late senator two children while married to another man—oh, what caviling!

I believe I may have omitted to mention it, but after the removal of his body, I visited the count's room and took away certain items to remember him by. One was his walking stick. It was ebony, with a silver tip and an ivory handle carved to look like a bear. Anyway, within seconds of spotting those stacks of twenty-dollar bills, I found myself standing over the policeman with the walking stick in my raised hand. He was still on the floor examining the letters and completely unaware of my presence. I hesitated for a moment, and then—the stick was snatched from my hand!

Mrs. Reese had snuck up behind me. I was surprised by her presence, but a good deal more surprised when she herself raised the stick! Like me, however, she found it much easier to entertain the idea of striking a policeman than to execute the act itself.

But not so the countess. Somehow she had managed to sneak in beside Mrs. Reese without either of us being aware. In one swift action, she seized the stick, raised it, and brought it down with a muffled thump.

"The trick is to hit the right spot with a moderate force," she explained. "Good lord, where'd that come from?" She'd seen the money.

"I thought I would use it for the funds," I told her.

"*Funds*," she said in a tone markedly lacking enthusiasm—then got down to business: "We must move quickly; we won't have much time."

As there were four stacks of bills, she took one for herself, gave one each to Mrs. Reese and myself, and then presented the last to Thomas, who had by then entered the room. Her largesse might seem an unnecessary act of generosity—after all, it *was* her kill. But I think a more accurate interpretation would be that she wished to bind us in the conspiracy. In the meantime, Mrs. Reese had picked up a letter lying beside the prostrate detective. It was in her hand, presumably one she'd written herself to Captain Dumont. What secrets it held, I would never know, as it instantly disappeared into her skirt along with her share of the loot.

The countess now doled out instructions: "Thomas, you and Mrs. Reese will carry the sergeant down to the billiard room, as quietly as humanly possible. Make sure the way is clear, then return here. Close up the trunk and take it to the porch of the Donovans' house next door. They're out of town, so no one will challenge you. I'll telephone an express company to pick it up there. Sesbania, you go into Mrs. Reese's room and start typing. We want it to seem as if she never left there."

The plan struck me as far too complicated, and under other circumstances, I might even have said so. But one gainsays the Countess von Schnurrenberger at one's peril. As Thomas and Mrs. Reese left carrying the body, I went into her room and sat down at the typewriter. The page in the machine was filled with numbers in a definite pattern. I couldn't make sense of it. But then I realized she'd been typing what she'd already worked out in pencil. So I just continued what she had started.

9

I heard people in the hall, but kept right on typing until Mrs. Reese returned.

"Did everything go as planned?" I asked.

"I think so. Harry's found him in the billiard room and is calling the doctor. I hope you didn't make a mess of my code."

"Is that what it is? I followed your sheet here. What's it mean?"

"Oh, just a sop for the sergeant and his Watson. I thought espionage might make a nice diversion."

"All this to protect Captain Dumont? Do you care for him that much?"

"Captain Dumont?" The query she delivered with playful incredulity; the coda came as chiding rebuke: "Don't overplay your hand, young lady."

She'd caught me unawares. "So you know...." My mind raced; which methodology would work best on her? Resigned remorse? "I'm glad, really.... But you don't think I did it on purpose?"

"No.... Of course not. I know you wouldn't." (Bull's-eye!) "You're a good girl—just one who did something *very* naughty."

"That's true, I suppose. But it wasn't me who set off the device."

"Then who did?"

I told her all about Mrs. Quinlan's visit and her exchange of letters with the count. Regrettably, however, I couldn't refrain from taking credit for their affair. She seemed rather shocked at my behavior, so I opted not to mention her own correspondence with the captain, or my sharing it with her husband.

"You really must learn to control your impulses," she told me. "And remember, the end does not always justify the means. It's all well and good teaching a man a lesson, but it must be done with some finesse."

"Like a chicken bone in his Charlotte Russe?"

"Well... a wife is allowed certain prerogatives an acquaintance is not. Let moderation be your watchword. Now go do what little girls do best."

"What's that?"

"Spy, of course. See what Harry is up to. Perhaps the sergeant is awake by now."

I'd felt earlier that Mrs. Reese's machinations were too scattershot to have a purpose. But I now realized that *was* her purpose. She'd spun the sergeant in one direction, then another, dizzying him with fabrications and insinuations. And all for my benefit. You might think this would have engendered some humility on my part. But to be perfectly honest, I'd come to think of it as my due.

I went down in time to encounter the doctor on his way out. It seems he had neglected to pick up his hat and coat on leaving after his last visit. I was so glad to be able to help him locate them, as was he—to the tune of three dollars and forty-three cents. All the money he had on him, in fact.

A police patrolman came to the house to tell Sergeant Lacy that Captain Dumont had not traveled to New York, as the countess had alleged. Then the sergeant, who had already been made aware of the fact, sent the man upstairs to guard the captain's trunk—the trunk which had previously been moved to the neighbors' porch.

After an agitated but fruitless search for it, the two detectives returned to the billiard room and considered the possibilities. The favorite theory of the sergeant was that Mr. Reese was the guilty party. He pulled out the letter I'd given him earlier that morning—the one supposedly from the captain to the count, instructing him to keep away from a woman who bore a strong resemblance to Mrs. Reese.

This sparked some concern in Mr. Reese, and it was then that he introduced the conjecture that the money in the trunk might have derived from the captain's winnings at games of chance. And that perhaps some gambler who felt himself cheated by the Frenchman had entered the house and knocked out the sergeant in order to retrieve the money he felt rightfully his. It sounded too flimsy a notion to stand on its own, so I thought I would lend it some support.

I took a pair of dice from a backgammon set in the parlor and then went out to the carriage house, where a tall ladder was stored. I somehow managed to bring it out to the yard, but couldn't raise it up to the count's window. Luckily, Thomas had seen me struggling and came to my aid. I do so hope we can find a manservant as handy as Thomas.

With the ladder in place, I raced back inside for lunch. The countess and Mrs. Reese were already at the table discussing a plan of their own to hide the secret code in the count's room. It involved a small chest the countess had confiscated earlier and no doubt relieved of anything she felt of value.

During the meal, I told the sergeant how I had found a ladder leaning just outside an open window in the count's room. I then presented him with the dice I said were lying on the floor there. The policeman was *most* interested.

But we weren't done with him yet. The countess asked if they'd located the count's private correspondence, or the little chest he kept it in. Not surprisingly, they had not.

After lunch, a new search was made of the count's room. The ladder was discovered leaning against the house, just as I had reported. And the small chest was found. It contained certain letters, some of them written in code.

The code was rather ingenious. It involved... Well, no good would be served by going into that now. One never knows when one might have use for an ingenious code....

That afternoon was spent quietly by Mr. Reese, as he decoded his wife's message, and noisily by the sergeant, as he slept off his meal. I saw no reason to subject myself to his bestial snorting, so I went up to my room and tallied my take from the captain's trunk. It amounted to more than $600! I thought at first that Mrs. Bradley deserved the bulk of it, as the Strothers would likely have some assets of their own. It then occurred to me, however, that being a not unattractive woman, she was better equipped to gain the esteem of the jury.

But this conundrum was short-lived. Mrs. Reese came to my room, and after closing the door sat down on the bed beside me.

"Are you really planning to give your money to Mrs. Bradley?"

"And the Strothers. Father said her trial could last a year, and be very expensive. I imagine theirs could be as well."

"Yes, I'm sure that's true."

"You don't want to keep the money, do you?"

"Not without knowing how the captain came by it."

"You mean, if he came by it immorally, you'd feel no compunction about keeping it?"

"Well, I wouldn't put it exactly like that.... But there's no way of knowing...."

"No. And no way of putting it back now.... Would you like to make a contribution?"

"Yes, I suppose I would. But..."

"Oh, you needn't worry. I *swear* it will *all* go to the funds."

"It's not that. I just would prefer that you not tell the countess."

"Of course not. She didn't share it with us out of kindness."

"What a curious child you are."

She then gave me her stack of bills and left the room. I wasn't sure how to interpret her choice of adjective, but decided she'd meant it as a compliment.

Not long afterward, I had a similar conversation with Thomas. He too left me a stack of bills. And he also made the request I not tell the countess. In his case, I assumed the contribution was motivated less by any pangs of guilt than by a genuine wish to reward me for ridding him of the twin villains, the count and Captain Dumont.

Before leaving, however, he consulted me about a new difficulty. It seemed the countess had become aware of Gustave's wanderings at night and had tasked Thomas with putting an end to them.

"Can't she simply ordain it?" I asked.

"Well, she could.... But the countess feels in his debt,

and would hate to offend Gustave.... He knows so much... about cooking."

"Yes, I'm sure he knows all the secrets of the kitchen." We both knew what we were speaking about, of course: chicken bones. "I think the soundest course would be for the woman to call it off."

"*Women,*" Thomas corrected.

"He has more than one lover?"

"Oh, yes. Often three or four at a time."

"Well, that makes things easier. Where does Gwenie fit in this?"

"She is his favorite. A rich young widow."

"Is she attractive?"

"In her way, perhaps. But she very much enjoys the pastries he brings her."

"He is very vain about his pastries, isn't he?" (Later that night, we would learn what a supreme understatement this was.)

Still having samples of Gwenie's penmanship, I had no trouble composing a letter to Gustave telling him that, though she longed to see him, she'd had enough of his pastries. What she wanted most, she told him, was a good Yorkshire pudding.

Then I composed several copies of an anonymous letter in her hand informing his other paramours of his infidelity and threatening them with exposure. While Thomas hand-delivered these, I went out and slid the note to Gustave under the back door.

That evening, the countess hosted a dinner party to which I was pointedly not invited.

"I think it would be best if you were to stay in your room," she told me—then proceeded to undermine her directive: "But *were* you to see or hear anything interesting, do be sure to get names."

While supping with the servants, I saw my forged letter still sitting on the floor of the back hall.

"What's that?" I asked, innocently.

"What?"

I went and picked up the letter. "It's for you, Gustave."

He took it, smiled, then stuffed it in a pocket.

The guests wouldn't be arriving for several hours, so at the conclusion of our meal, I returned to my room to work on the problem of how to allocate the windfall.

It surprised me when I found that Thomas's contribution was short by some hundred dollars. The stacks were all quite equal-appearing when removed from the trunk. I was hurt he hadn't simply confided in me. But when I discovered Mrs. Reese, too, had shorted me—she'd replaced a good many of her twenties with smaller bills—my reaction was more nuanced. I hadn't found her performance quite convincing and was relieved to learn I'd not entirely misread her. There was little doubt, her conveyance was meant more as a bribe than a contribution. She had to be wondering what I knew of her correspondence with Captain Dumont. Nevertheless, she'd given me almost three hundred dollars, and since I'd already decided to put away a like portion of my own stack for unforeseen contingencies, I thought it best to be magnanimous and not point out the discrepancy.

The countess was renowned for the extravagance of her affairs, but until that night, I had no idea how extravagant. Champagne flowed like water—and so did the bourbon, scotch, gin, rum, and vodka. In fact, the only liquid that didn't was water.

With Thomas acting as barman, Geneviève and Herr

Kirsch brought out the endless stream of platters Gustave kept full of delicacies savory and sweet. While I, darting from cubbyhole to keyhole to drapery, took notes. For us, all was busyness.

The guests themselves, however, were not so energetic, nor particularly diverting. I observed drunken congressmen playing billiards with young women not their wives, eavesdropped on their wives confessing their own indiscretions to their sister wives, and watched as a senator fell under the sway of the countess. But a little of that sort of thing goes a long way. I quickly tired of the spectacle and went up to bed, stopping only to take a peek at a tryst underway in the late count's bedchamber. Here, at least, there was no lack of energy. The lighting was dim, but the pair's athleticism more than compensated for the lack of detail. Some of their contortions seemed to defy the law of gravity.

Unfortunately, just as things were getting really steamy, Mr. Reese arrived. So consumed had I become with the spectacle before me, I let out an involuntary cry when he came out of nowhere and surprised me. Then, a moment later, he was discovered in turn. A half-naked lady emerged from the room and made a beeline for the bathroom.

I slept quite soundly that night. At least, until sometime early the next morning, when Geneviève could be heard screaming in the hall. "It's murder!" she shrieked.

You may be sure, she didn't need to shriek twice to get me out of bed.

10

Whatever the circumstances, I don't consider myself any more culpable in Herr Kirsch's death than in that of the count. Nevertheless, I will relate the sequence of events—as told to me by Geneviève—and you may judge for yourself.

Sometime that busy evening, when he had a brief moment to himself, Gustave read the letter I'd composed from Gwenie. The news that she had tired of the prideful cook's pastries cut him like a knife; and with her suggestion that he make her a Yorkshire pudding, she had given the knife a painful twist. He'd already been partaking of the champagne rather freely; now he redoubled those efforts.

By the time the last of the guests had departed, and the servants were free to clear the tables, Gustave was in his cups, wallowing in a drunken mire of self-pity and aggrievement. Why Herr Kirsch took this occasion to offer his unenthusiastic assessment of the French cook's strudel, we will never know. Surely, the result surprised even him.

I remember the tableau in the kitchen quite vividly. It isn't often one sees a man lying on the floor with a meat cleaver planted in his chest (though the calmness with which the countess took in the scene led me to wonder if it held the same novelty for her).

This time, there was no question it was murder; nor was there any doubt who committed the crime, or of his intentions. Nonetheless, any talk of calling in the police was cut short by the countess. Gustave was sent to his room like a disobedient child, while Thomas and Mr. Reese were dispatched in the auto with the corpse riding in back. Later, I learned they disposed of it in the canal which runs through Georgetown. A poor choice, Thomas agreed, but one born of necessity.

A few days before, I'd seen Herr Kirsch speaking with some men in an automobile a block or two from the house. He didn't seem to be enjoying the interview and I had wondered how to account for the situation. Not so now. When I found Sergeant Lacy at the breakfast table the next morning, I spun a yarn about observing Herr Kirsch being abducted by suspicious-looking foreigners out on the street.

"I believe they might have been Russian agents," I told him. "Or perhaps German."

I hoped this might harmonize nicely with Mrs. Reese's coded messages. And apparently it did—at least, to the sergeant's satisfaction.

That evening, he enumerated his conclusions to Mr. Reese. First, Dumont and the count were both spies. Second, the Frenchman had built the contraption to thwart his rival. Third, the valet's disappearance could be attributed to the postmaster general's coachman—a bizarre theory due partly to a small typographical error on my part. And with that, he unceremoniously closed his investigation of the count's death.

The question of who set off the Frenchman's machine was set aside as irrelevant, since whoever it was had almost certainly done so unwittingly. (Nevertheless, the detective left little doubt he still suspected Mrs. Reese.)

The next day was the 24th and I spent it amongst the barbaric hordes doing some last-minute Christmas shopping. The countess's taste ran to the highly sophisti-cated and narrowly selective and—outside of another volume of French erotica—I was at a loss as to what to get her. But I remembered that the year before my father had suggested giving her a nutcracker. (An idea quickly squelched by my blushing mother.) I didn't understand the joke at the time, of course, only that there was one. And I assumed any joke beyond my understanding was probably a very good one. So nutcracker it was.

For Thomas I bought a small volume on the com-posing of love letters. It was pretty tame stuff, but one needs to work up to such imagery as "*a bubbling river of Aphrodite's rich drippings....*"

For Gustave, I bought a knife sharpener, and for Geneviève, a properly shaped darning egg.

To Mr. Reese I gave his own hat and coat, wrapped up quite elaborately, with red and green bows. And for his wife, I made copies of Gwenie's inimitable corre-spondence (the originals are in my scrapbook). I thought these might prove useful in her novel writing. I gave her a second gift as well—this one unbeknownst to her.

I was touched by how she had expended so much ef-fort obscuring my part in the affair of the count's death. What I don't believe she realized was that her husband had likewise deduced my involvement, or at least sus-pected it. He dropped repeated hints, in his droll, teasing way, until the day the sergeant dropped the investigation. We were approaching one another on the stairs and he stopped.

"Well, it looks as if you'll get away with it," he told me.

"Get away with what? I don't know what you're talk-ing about."

"Uh-huh. Just don't let it go to your head."

"You don't think I killed the count, do you?"

"Let's just say, if you'd gone to Europe with your parents, he'd still be alive and well."

There was no refuting that. "You won't tell the countess?"

"No, but I wouldn't be so sure she hasn't figured it out herself."

"I don't suppose it would do much good to tell you it wasn't done consciously."

"Mmm, maybe a little. But next time…"

"Don't worry. Are you going to tell Mrs. Reese?"

"Are you sure she hasn't figured it out?"

"That's just it. She has. But she's gone to such a great deal of effort to throw you and the sergeant off the track. Couldn't you *not* tell her? It could be sort of a Christmas present."

He gave me a queer look. "Sure." Then he proceeded up the stairs.

The countess, Mrs. Reese, and I were to go out for a long series of events on Christmas Eve, and it was as I was preparing that Thomas came to my room. He told me that though my campaign for foiling Gustave's amours had been effective, he had already met a new young woman.

"She works for the florist. She delivered some flowers for tomorrow's table and Gustave insisted she try the torte he'd made for coffee. Now, she is *his*.…"

"It *was* a very fine torte," I noted.

"Yes, and tomorrow there will be another, and another girl.…"

"What if he were to settle on one woman? Would that satisfy the countess?"

"Only if he were to remain here with her."

"Is there really nothing between him and Geneviève? She's quite attractive, and is very appreciative of his pastries."

"The countess has always frowned on such goings-on."

"Yes, but what if it weren't a mere backstairs affair? What if they married?"

"Oh, Gustave marry? I don't think he could ever allow himself to be tied down."

"And Geneviève?"

"Well, of course she has feelings for him, whether he knows it or not. She often waits up for him when he goes out."

"I thought it was Herr Kirsch she was pining for?"

"Him? No, never."

"I saw them flirting all the time."

"Oh, that was at the wish of Madam. She didn't trust the valet and wanted him watched."

"So it's just a matter of winning over Gustave," I said. "Or at least forcing his hand."

"Forcing his hand?"

"Just leave it to me."

The perfume, *Deux nuits d'excès,* was still in the possession of Mrs. Reese. For reasons of expediency, I haven't before conveyed the impression it made on her. Suffice it to say, it was a conspicuous one. The first night she wore it was the one during which Herr Kirsch met his maker. Mr. Reese was sent out with Thomas to dispose of the corpse, leaving her alone. But not for long, apparently. I peeked in their room early the next morning, before her husband had returned, and saw her and Geneviève in what can only be called a compromising position. They were asleep, seemingly exhausted. I only wish I'd thought to bring my camera along.

On the second night, her husband was again sent out of the house. Geneviève, perhaps feeling penitent, lent the insatiable woman one of her ill-shaped darning eggs in lieu of her person. What use was made of it, I could not say for certain. She slept with the light off and the curtains closed. But from the telltale tones emanating from her room, I surmised she knew all about darning in the dark.

Since she had by Christmas Eve used up her *Deux nuits d'excès* (one way or another), I commandeered the perfume (and the misshapen darning egg) and brought it (but not the egg) to Geneviève's room. After taking a drop or two for myself, I placed the vial on her table (and confiscated the remaining of her misshapen darning eggs).

As I mentioned, the countess, Mrs. Reese, and I had a full evening of events, stretching until well past midnight. So Geneviève would be alone in the house with Thomas and Gustave. Now it was just a matter of Thomas making himself scarce when the time was ripe.

Things, however, did not go as planned, for two reasons: Gustave drank himself into incapacity and I had forgotten Mr. Reese. What occurred before our arrival home, I will never be sure. But from the sheepish mien of the maid the next day, I'm in no doubt it was *something*.

That was Christmas Day, and a rather subdued one at that. We all rose late and conversation at the dinner table was hushed. Even I was quiet. I'd drunk my first wine the evening before and was now suffering my first hangover. As soon as dessert had been cleared, Thomas took the Reeses to the station—the countess's gift to them being two tickets for home.

This would be Geneviève's second night with the perfume and I was determined that nothing would be left to chance. I had, naturally, appropriated *Gamiani* from Mrs. Reese's luggage. Now I put it to good use. I wrote a little dedication in Geneviève's hand and placed the book on the Frenchman's pillow. That evening, Thomas shared two bottles of champagne (and no more) with the cook and maid. He then sent them to their rooms.

The next morning, I revealed to the countess my scheme. After much discussion, she agreed an in-house marriage might be best for all concerned. And so she, Thomas, and I went up to Gustave's room, expecting to surprise the pair draped in each other's arms and sound asleep. Instead, they were still at it.

When they emerged from the bower sometime after six that evening, the countess toasted their betrothal and that was that. They now have two girls and a little boy and live in an apartment just around the corner from their mistress.

The next day, my parents returned, and Jessie the day after that. They were all three astonished at the sums I'd raised for Mrs. Bradley and the Strother brothers. I'm sure I was quite insufferable for a period, my head swelled by my many triumphs.

Then, some three weeks later, my mother spotted an item in the social column: the latest Count von Schnurrenberger und Kesselheim—a nineteen-year-old university student who was said to be both an able athlete and an accomplished musician—had arrived for a stay with his step-aunt.

After Geneviève's second night, I took possession of

the precious last drops of the formidable perfume. The bottle has since remained unopened and will continue so until tomorrow. I do hope you're up to it. If not, Geneviève's misshapen darning eggs stand always at the ready.